# CARNIVAL OF MONSTERS

*It was like no dog that Billy had ever seen. The torso and front legs looked more human than canine, lean and muscular beneath a coat of black fur. The front paws were like elongated hands ending in deadly talons. The back legs were totally dog-like though, and so was the tail swishing from side to side between them. On its back were a pair of leathery wings. The head was that of a monstrous hound, with swept back ears, and a mouth full of yellowing teeth. Billy caught a flash of the creature's eyes. They were fiercely intelligent and they blazed with red fire.*

**ANDREW BEASLEY** was born in Hertfordshire, and has spent most of his life with his nose buried in a book. Andrew works as a primary school teacher, and is also the author of *The Battles of Ben Kingdom* series: the first book, *The Claws of Evil*, was nominated for the Carnegie Medal. He lives in Cornwall with his wife and their two children, Ben and Lucy.

*For Amanda*
*Best. Sister. Ever.*

First published in the UK in 2017 by Usborne Publishing Ltd., Usborne House, 83-85 Saffron Hill, London EC1N 8RT, England. www.usborne.com

Text copyright © Andrew Beasley, 2017

Cover illustration by Manuel Šumberac.
Illustration copyright © Usborne Publishing Ltd.

Lyrics from *Daddy Wouldn't Buy Me a Bow-wow* by Joseph Tabrar (1892).

A CIP catalogue record for this book is available from the British Library.

ISBN 9781474906937 JFMAMJJ SOND/17 03956/1

Printed in the UK.

# S.C.R.E.A.M.
## CARNIVAL OF MONSTERS

# ANDREW BEASLEY

USBORNE

# ALL THE FUN OF THE FAIR

"We're in trouble, aren't we?"

For a moment Bunny Smallbone didn't reply to her younger brother, Arthur. They both knew the answer: they weren't just in trouble, they were in *big* trouble.

But only if they got caught.

"Keep quiet, pudding head," Bunny hissed as they sneaked down the country lane to their house. "We'll be fine as long as Father doesn't find out."

"What if the monsters follow us home?" gasped Arthur.

Bunny stopped and took her younger brother by the shoulders. "Listen to me," she said, talking firmly but kindly. "There are no such things as monsters."

"But we've seen them!" said Arthur, breathless with emotion. "The vampire and the minotaur and the ghosts and the Amazing Man-Bat!" His lip trembled. "And the Devil himself."

"It was a carnival," Bunny explained. "Pretend. Play-acting. People in costumes, dressed up to scare us. That's all."

"Those horrible clowns!"

"Just people with their faces painted. Nothing for a big boy like you to be afraid of."

Arthur put on his brave face.

"Try not to think about it," said Bunny, taking her brother's hand and pulling him onwards down the lane. It was good advice, but easier said than done. Most of the horrors they had witnessed at Dr Vindicta's Carnival of Monsters *weren't* that easy to explain. Bunny had seen two ghosts dancing onstage, a husband and wife spinning in slow circles while their hollow bodies passed *through* the table and chairs. Of course it had to be an illusion — but if it was all just make-up and make-believe, then why was her flesh creeping?

Bunny's pace quickened. She was suddenly anxious to be home. A fat autumn moon hung in the black velvet sky like a dollop of cream. It gave just enough light to make the shadows darker. The hedgerow seemed to be alive. Unseen insects chirped and hummed. In the field beyond the hedge, something was snuffling through the undergrowth, coughing like an old man. A hedgehog, Bunny told herself. Or a badger.

She stole a glance over her shoulder. The shadows moved. It was her imagination, of course. They weren't being followed. There was nothing there. They were alone in the lane. Quite alone.

"Hurry up, Arthur," she snapped, dragging him along now.

"So there's no such thing as monsters?"

"No."

"No werewolves or mummies or zombies?"

"No."

"What about the Hobb-Hound?"

Bunny paused. The Hobb-Hound. The demon dog that fed on fear. Every child in Hobb's End knew the legend. She shuddered. "Superstitious nonsense."

"That's good," said Arthur. "Otherwise it would be really scary."

"What would?"

"This," said Arthur. "Walking home. In the dark. With something following us."

They lived in the countryside, and the countryside was *always* full of noises that couldn't be explained. The animal had been following them for a little while. Bunny could hear its breath, and now its footfall. Whatever it was, it sounded bigger than a hedgehog, that was for sure. Much bigger.

*Still, not far to go now*, she told herself. She could be brave enough for both of them until they were back in their house with the door firmly shut. Just keep walking and don't look back.

*"Beware the monster of the night,"* sang Arthur, *"that feeds on vengeance, hate and fright.*

*"It searches far, it searches near, it sniffs you out and smells your fear.*

*"So when the sun comes out to play, all the boys have gone away,*

*"Taken swiftly in the night, when the Hobb-Hound takes to flight!"*

"Stop it!" said Bunny, her heart thumping like a frightened rabbit's. Why was he chanting that stupid rhyme?

"But you said the legend of the Hobb-Hound isn't real," Arthur protested.

"I know what I said, but...but we want to get in without Father knowing, don't we? So we need to be as quiet as mice. All right?"

"All right," said Arthur.

In the lane behind them a twig snapped. "Hurry up," said Bunny.

The house was only a little way ahead now. Thank goodness! "Look," said Bunny as they turned the corner and saw the imposing outline of Smallbone Manor. "The light is on in Father's study, so if we sneak in through the back door—"

"And straight up the stairs to bed, I know," Arthur finished, "we might just get away with it!"

"Remember, whatever you do, don't mention the carnival."

In the darkness of the lane something growled.

Arthur squeezed Bunny's hand tight enough to make her knuckles pop.

"Bunny," squeaked Arthur.

"I heard it too," said Bunny. "It's just a dog."

"Just a dog."

"How about we have a race, Arthur?" said Bunny,

swallowing her panic. "Let's see who can get home the fastest."

The thing in the shadows snarled.

"RUN!" shouted Bunny.

All their plans about getting into the house undiscovered disappeared in an instant. They ran inside at top speed, panting and sweating and slammed the front door behind them with enough force to wake the dead. Arthur came to a skidding halt on the tiled hall floor, right in front of their father, Major Smallbone, waiting with his arms crossed.

"And where have you two been?" Major Smallbone bellowed.

"The carnival!" Arthur blurted out. "Bunny made me go!"

A second passed while the major's nostrils flared like a bull's and his moustache did an angry dance on his top lip. "BUNNY!" he bellowed. "So you've been to the carnival, have you? How dare you go there after I said you couldn't!"

Now that Bunny was safely home, she felt the warm embrace of relief as her fears began to drift away. Father was cross – it was so reassuringly normal! Major "Tiger" Smallbone stood in front of his children and glared at them as if they were two of his soldiers who had done something unforgivable, like letting their rifles go rusty or forgetting the words to the national anthem. His lips were pinched so tightly, he looked as if he had been sucking a lemon. His hairy nostrils flared. His large ears, which stuck out like an elephant's, went as red as tomatoes. He looked slightly ridiculous, and in spite of everything Bunny struggled with the urge to giggle nervously.

"I'm sorry, Father," she said, keeping her eyes down. "It was just meant to be a bit of fun."

"Fun? FUN!" If the major's head had been made of dynamite it would have exploded by now. "I never had fun when *I* was a child," he boomed.

"But I'm NOT a child!" snapped Bunny, a spark of defiance bristling inside her. "And I'm not one of your soldiers either. I don't have to take your orders, Major!"

"Well, I..." Major Smallbone deflated slightly, like the last balloon when the party was over. Bunny felt a pang of compassion for him then. None of them had been the same since Mother had died, quite suddenly and unfairly, one rainy day two years ago. Bunny had been a child of fifteen then, but she was a young woman now.

Major Smallbone regained his composure. "Bed!" he snapped. "At the double!"

Obediently Bunny and Arthur scurried up the stairs. But Bunny was smiling by the time she reached the top and arrived on the landing, dark corridors stretching out to the left and right. "Yes, Sir!" she whispered.

Arthur still appeared shaken, though, and Bunny gave him a quick hug. He squirmed out of it but he was smiling too by the time he escaped. Arthur was ten but somehow he always seemed younger at bedtime and Bunny decided to get him settled in his room first. While he slipped out of his clothes and into his nightshirt, she lit the candle beside his bed and turned back the sheet. She kissed him softly on the cheek and he wormed down beneath his quilt until only his eyes and the top of his head were showing. "Sweet dreams, Arthur, don't be afraid. There's no such thing as monsters," she said as she smoothed his unruly hair. "Except for the ogre downstairs."

Arthur laughed at her joke, but Bunny could see that he was still uneasy. "Don't worry," she said. "Father won't be grumpy for long."

"I know," said Arthur. "But..." He left the sentence unfinished but his gaze flicked towards the window and the shadows in the lane.

"It was just a show," said Bunny. "Nothing at the

carnival was real, and the Hobb-Hound is just an old story that parents tell to scallywags like you." She kissed him again. "I'm next door if you need me. Now close those eyes and get some sleep."

Bunny left her brother and went along the corridor to her room. Once her own candle was burning merrily, she threw herself down backwards onto the bed, a huge grin on her lips. Father was angry with them, but that was nothing new. As Bunny remembered the dizzying rides and the sticky sweet toffee apples and the wonders she had seen, she had no doubt that it was worth getting told off for.

She couldn't be bothered to get into her nightdress yet and so she lay with her head on her soft pillow, reliving every moment of her adventure. Bunny couldn't remember ever having more fun than she had had at Dr Vindicta's Carnival of Monsters. No. Perhaps "fun" wasn't the right word. Bunny had laughed, that was true, but she had screamed more! The rides and the candyfloss. The clowns and the coconuts. The Minotaur! The ghosts! The Wheel of the Devil! It had all been so gloriously thrilling and wonderful and well...*scary*, but Bunny had never felt more alive! Hobb's End was such a boring place; nothing had ever happened there. Until now.

The carnival was in town for two more days and Bunny decided that she was *definitely* going back, regardless of what her father said – the old stick-in-the-mud.

Bunny was feeling rather pleased with herself when a sudden chill filled her room. She shivered. Perhaps she would get ready for bed after all. It was getting late, and there was nothing quite as cosy as pulling the blankets right up to your chin.

She went to her dressing table. As she reached for her hairbrush, the candle on the table fluttered. A coil of blue smoke curled upwards as the flame sputtered and died. Strange… Placing the brush down, Bunny put out her hand for the matches…and froze.

There was something outside her room.

Not in the corridor. *But outside her window something was moving.*

Bunny wanted to scream. She wanted to run to her father. But she couldn't. Her voice was trapped and her legs had turned to jelly. All she could do was watch and wait. She told herself a comforting lie: *It's probably only an owl.*

Long seconds passed, each one felt like for ever. Had she imagined it?

A black shape passed Bunny's window.

*No!*

Sudden and shocking. Large enough to block out the light of the moon and plunge her room into darkness. A gasp escaped Bunny's lips.

There were plenty of owls in the woods around Hobb's End, but this was not an owl. Owls were never so big.

Arthur's scream pierced the night and shocked Bunny into action, like a slap across the face. Bunny knew all the noises that her brother made. The coughs, the sneezes, the snores, the deafening farts. The sound that Arthur was making now was a cry of pure terror. Bunny pounded out of her room. Panic-stricken, she fumbled with the handle of Arthur's door and lost precious moments before she flung it open and burst into his room. She froze again as her mind struggled to make sense of what was happening.

It was all over in the blink of an eye.

Arthur's windows were open wide. Bunny caught a fleeting glimpse of a terrifying shape filling the gap. Blacker than black. Darker than the darkest night. Bunny couldn't make out what it was, but she could hear the horrible thing breathing in short, rasping gasps. She winced at the stench which spilled into the room – worse even than Arthur's morning breath, and that was saying something. Two things Bunny knew for certain: this *creature* was evil. And, most terrible of all, it had her little brother in its grasp.

Bunny saw Arthur squirming to get free. The creature glared at her with blazing red eyes which burned into her memory like hot coals. Then, before Bunny could react or even say a single word, the creature launched itself into the night with a flap of its wings, carrying Arthur with it. Bunny was left stunned, with Arthur's last words worming in her ears. *"Help me, Bunny. Please!"*

Bunny tried to shout for her father, but her words shrivelled to dust in her mouth. *It couldn't be*, she told herself. *It's just a legend.* But try as she might the sinister lines of the rhyme kept running through her mind:

*Beware the monster of the night,*

*that feeds on vengeance, hate and fright.*

*It searches far, it searches near,*

*it sniffs you out and smells your fear.*

*So when the sun comes out to play,*

*all the boys have gone away,*

*Taken swiftly in the night,*

*when the Hobb-Hound takes to flight!*

# CHAPTER ONE

## ALL ABOARD THE GHOST TRAIN

"Something's died in here," said Billy Flint.

Charlotte Steel's ears pricked up. Billy was her partner in the most secret department of the Metropolitan Police Force. On top of that, he had a unique gift for sensing the supernatural realm. When Billy spoke about spirits, Charley listened.

"What are you detecting?" asked Charley, looking around their train carriage. Was the thin, pale-faced man hiding behind his newspaper really a vampire? Or how about the shrivelled old woman, was she an animated corpse? Charley shuddered. Perhaps the seat next to hers wasn't empty after all? Was she sitting next to a ghost?

"What is it, Billy?"

"I dunno," said Billy, a cheeky grin forming on his lips. "Can't you smell it too?"

Charley wrinkled her nose. The air was certainly a little "ripe", although good manners prevented her from saying so out loud. Billy Flint was less bothered by etiquette.

He stood up and examined the soles of his boots. Satisfied that he hadn't stepped in anything unpleasant, he continued his search. "Either something died in here or you've let one go on the quiet and owe me a serious apology, Duchess."

Charley wasn't a duchess, although her father was richer than a lot of dukes. In many ways Charley couldn't be more different from her partner. Charley Steel had been to Buckingham Palace and had tea with Queen Victoria. Billy Flint had been to Newgate Prison to visit his uncle, Jonno "the Knuckles" Flint. If it hadn't been for Luther Sparkwell, the founder and only other member of S.C.R.E.A.M., their worlds would never have touched…unless one of Billy's relatives robbed one of Charley's.

"He who smelt it dealt it," said Charley, matching Billy's grin with a perfect white smile of her own.

Determined to find the source of the smell, Billy lifted the leather-padded seat. Underneath, in a nest of chewed leather and horsehair matting, Billy found a dead and half-decomposed rat. Unflinching, he picked it up by the tail, waved it around triumphantly, then lowered the window and tossed it outside. The other passengers in the carriage saw the rat and decided that they might be more comfortable in a different compartment, leaving Billy and Charley alone.

With the smell of rotting rat fading but not forgotten, Billy nevertheless opened his satchel and pulled out some sandwiches wrapped in greaseproof paper. "So tell me again," he said, hungrily tucking into his cheese and pickle. "What are we up against this time?"

Charley withdrew the red case file from her own satchel. The S.C.R.E.A.M. insignia was stamped on the front. The initials stood for Supernatural Crimes, Rescues, Emergencies And Mysteries. The S.C.R.E.A.M. squad investigated the cases that would make other police officers run a mile.

"We don't have much to go on," Charley admitted. "But we received a telegram this morning and Luther thought it was serious enough to put us on the next train."

Luther Sparkwell was their commanding officer in S.C.R.E.A.M. Most people didn't take Luther seriously on first impression, mainly because the man had hair like a scarecrow and the eyebrows of an angry badger. Luther also had the dress sense of a tramp and would stand a good chance of winning if he ever decided to enter in a "Be Rude to Random People" championship. However, in the field of paranormal studies and occult lore, Luther Sparkwell was a genius.

"Who was the telegram from?" asked Billy.

"Bunny Smallbone," said Charley.

"Bunny?" Billy sniggered. "Is that even a name? Rabbit used to be dinner in my house."

Charlotte Steel gave Billy *the look*. Obediently Billy wiped the grin from his face. "Bunny happens to be an old school friend," she explained.

"Sorry," said Billy. "Any friend of yours is a friend of mine." He ran his hand through his hair. "Pretty is she, this Bunny?"

"Yes," said Charley. "Pretty clever. Pretty independent."

"Pretty much like you."

Charley smiled. "Let's get back to the case, shall we?" She handed the telegram to Billy and he read it aloud.

POST OFFICE TELEGRAPHS

HANDED IN AT: HOBB'S END       RECEIVED AT: WESTMINSTER

Dear Charley,
I do not know who else to turn to.
A monster has kidnapped my brother.
Please help.
Bunny Smallbone

"Doesn't give us much to go on, does it?" said Billy.

"No," Charley admitted. "But I trust Bunny. If she says it was a 'monster', she means it."

"Not a job for the regular police, then," said Billy.

"Quite," Charley agreed as she flicked through the case notes that Luther had provided for them. "Ooh," she said, her clear blue eyes lighting up with interest as she pulled out a sheet covered in Luther's untidy scrawl. "What have we here?" Charley read quickly. "There's a local legend."

"Isn't there always?" said Billy, rolling his eyes.

"Yes," said Charley, "but not like this." She scanned the page. "Bunny lives in the town of Hobb's End—"

"Hobb," interrupted Billy, "the old English word for the Devil?"

"Yes."

"You take me to all the nice places."

"Apparently Hobb's End was once terrorized by a creature known as the Hobb-Hound," Charley continued.

"Never heard of it," said Billy.

"Not many people have outside of Hobb's End," said Charley, "even Luther's notes are a bit sketchy. It seems to be some sort of demon dog." Charley read on. Then she paused, sucking on her teeth. "Listen to this: *Beware the monster of the night, that feeds on vengeance, hate and fright.*

"*It searches far, it searches near, it sniffs you out and smells your fear.*

"*So when the sun comes out to play, all the boys have gone away,*

"*Taken swiftly in the night, when the Hobb-Hound takes to flight!*"

"Any actual *evidence* though?" said Billy. "How many local legends have we investigated that turned out to be superstitious nonsense mixed with hysteria?"

"Remember the Beast of Bodmin Moor?" said Charley.

"What a gorgeous animal she was." He smiled at the memory. "Not a monster at all."

"Although it is still a mystery how a black panther came to be roaming free in Cornwall."

"So, has Luther been able to dig up any confirmed sightings of the beast of Hobb's End?"

"Nothing conclusive," said Charley. "The reports we have of the few alleged incidents aren't very convincing—"

"Because sightings of demon dogs could easily be sightings of…well, just dogs."

"Precisely." Charley nodded.

"So what you're saying is that we haven't really got any idea what we're up against at all?"

"What's new?" said Charley, her smile stretching from ear to ear. "The unknown is what we do best."

As the train rocked and juddered down the track out of London and towards the West Country, Charley and Billy worked their way through the files that Luther Sparkwell had prepared for them. There were police documents on child disappearances going back decades, as well as several ancient books on demonology and every possible dog-related myth, plus a small amount of information on the Hobb-Hound and the sleepy town of Hobb's End.

Billy was a skim-reader. He flicked through the pages, looking at the pictures and snatching out the juiciest paragraphs. Charley, on the other hand, was a surgeon when it came to books. Her mind was precise and scalpel-sharp, cutting through the gristle to get to the facts.

At Bristol they had to change trains and switch to the small branch line that would take them to Hobb's End.

"Can I assist you, Miss?" asked the guard, as Charley manoeuvred her wicker wheelchair within the tight confines of the train.

"Yes, please," said Charley, "that's kind."

Together with the guard, Billy helped Charley out of one train and then onto another.

Safely on board, Charley noticed that the guard was staring at her.

"Childhood polio," she said. "In case you were wondering."

Billy shook his head. "He's not looking at your chair."

Charley looked down and saw that the blanket covering her legs had slipped to reveal the gun which she carried with her at all times. "Oh," said Charley. "Sorry."

She picked up the small pistol which was lying on

her lap. "It's a British Webley five-shot pocket revolver, nickel plate with wooden grips," she explained airily, holding the gun in the air. "The British 'Bull Dog'." She spun the chamber while the guard watched in stunned silence. "Bark and bite!" Charley laughed. "You might be interested to know that it is the same make of gun which was used to assassinate the American President, James Garfield, back in 1881."

"He was killed at a train station," Billy chipped in. "A lot like this one."

"Don't know if it works on demon dogs," said Charley, still admiring her gun. "But I guess we'll find out soon enough."

The guard's mouth was hanging slightly open. His face had gone a queasy white. "Demon dogs?"

"Like dogs," said Charley. "Only demonic."

"You are the strangest people I've ever met," said the guard and with that he suddenly found that he urgently needed to be somewhere else and hurried away.

Charley and Billy shared a smile. "You love this, don't you?" said Billy.

"Solving crimes, rescuing children, defeating supernatural villains." Charley grinned. "What's not to love?"

# CHAPTER TWO

# NOT A HAPPY BUNNY

"Charley Steel! It really *is* you!"

"Bunny Smallbone," said Charley warmly. "How long has it been?"

Bunny had been waiting for them on the platform. She looked uncomfortably from Charley's face to her wheelchair. "A long time," said Bunny with obvious sadness. "I didn't know," she said. "I'm sorry."

"Don't be," said Charley, changing the conversation. "Let me introduce my partner. Bunny Smallbone, this is Detective Constable William Flint."

"Billy," said Billy, putting out his hand for Bunny

to shake. "Charmed, I'm sure."

"Very professional," said Charley with a mock sigh. "Come on."

Bunny had changed too in the years since she and Charley had shared a room at boarding school. Her friend's hair was still a warm chestnut brown, but now it was beautifully curled – not the tangled mess it had once been – and her "bunny" buck teeth were straight and perfectly white. She had a carriage ready for them and after they had loaded their luggage they were on their way.

"Right," said Charley. "Tell us the whole story."

"Oh, it's terrible," said Bunny, holding her face in her hands. "Arthur's missing and the police won't listen to me at all." Her big brown eyes welled with tears.

"*We're* listening," said Billy, his heart going out to her. He passed her his handkerchief. "It's clean," he said. "Well, cleanish."

Bunny took it and tried a brave smile. "I don't know where to start," she said.

"From the beginning," said Charley, her notepad open and pencil poised. "Any detail might be important."

Bunny composed herself with a deep breath. "Last night Arthur and I were coming home from Dr Vindicta's Carnival of Monsters—"

"The what?" spluttered Billy.

"It's a travelling funfair," Bunny explained. "You know, rides and sideshows."

"And the monsters?"

"A gimmick, I suppose you'd call it. All the carnival folk wear scary costumes and most of the attractions are designed to give you a fright."

"We'll need to know every ride you went on, anyone you spoke to, each attraction you saw," said Charley.

"Why?"

"Because it might be a coincidence that your brother was kidnapped when all these strangers were in Hobb's End. But it's equally possible that there's a link," said Billy. "We have to check every possible line of enquiry."

"It's a bit of a blur," said Bunny. "Arthur wanted candyfloss, and we spoke to the vampire when we gave him our money."

"Vampire?" said Billy.

"Candyfloss seller in a costume," said Charley. "Try to keep up."

"We went through the Minotaur's Maze of Mirrors, and saw the Ghost Dance. Then Arthur needed a wee and I had to hold his candyfloss while he nipped behind one of the tents." Bunny smiled at the memory but then her lip began to tremble. "I'm sorry," she said. "These last few hours have been…so hard. I feel as if I'm going mad."

"Nobody understands that better than we do," said Charley. "Believe me. I'm a scientist, so when I had to start dealing with ghosts and the supernatural –" she shook her head – "let's just say I had some serious thinking to do."

Bunny sniffed into Billy's handkerchief. "After that we watched the Amazing Man-Bat fly through the air, and then we visited the Wheel of the Devil. Then we ran out of money and it was getting late, so we set off home."

Charley wrote all this down. "What happened then?"

"We'd both been so excited at the carnival, but the walk home was creepy."

"Creepy how?" asked Billy.

"We felt as if we were being followed," said Bunny.

"Someone from the funfair?"

"It didn't sound like a person."

"And did you see anything?"

"It was too dark," said Bunny, "and we were running by the time we got home. Father was furious and sent us straight to our rooms." She sighed. "I couldn't blame him, we had been out against his strict instructions.

Anyway, Arthur and I went upstairs, and that was when…"

"When it happened?" Charley finished quietly.

Bunny nodded. "I heard a scream from Arthur's room and ran straight in."

"I know this is difficult," said Charley, "but whatever you remember might bring us closer to finding Arthur."

"It was so quick, I don't really know what I saw. Just an impression…" Bunny took a long, deep breath through her nose. "The windows were open and the space was filled by a black shape I couldn't make out." All the blood drained from Bunny's face as she relived those horrible seconds. "It had arms and claws – I know that because the creature was holding Arthur so tightly. Arthur was struggling but the thing was too strong."

"What else?"

"The candle had blown out, and it was so dark…I saw sharp teeth, glinting, and the most horrible red eyes, burning like fire. Then it was gone. It flew away carrying Arthur. I was petrified, Charley. This *thing* had my little brother and I stood there like an idiot."

"There's nothing you could have done," said Billy.

"I know," said Bunny, "but I could have *tried*."

It was late afternoon when the carriage drew up at

a large red-brick country house. It looked like a picture postcard; there were even roses around the door. "Here we are," said Bunny.

"The scene of the crime," said Billy.

"My home," said Bunny quietly.

# CHAPTER THREE

# THE WRONG ARM OF THE LAW

Billy unloaded Charley's wheelchair, and then helped her down from the carriage. Charley brushed off her tweed jacket and smoothed back her long red hair, fixing it in place with a length of black ribbon.

Bunny led them into the house. There were voices coming from one of the front rooms. "Father must have a visitor," said Bunny. "It sounds like Constable Dunstable. Perhaps he'll be able to help us after all."

"I wouldn't count on it," said Billy. "Our methods are a bit different from the local police's. They tend not to like it when we suggest 'a ghost did it' or anything like that."

"Be fair," said Charley. "Constable Dunstable might be the exception."

"I'll tell you what," said Billy. "You make the introductions, Bunny. Charley, you work your charm on Constable Dunstable, and I'll have a look around upstairs, if that's all right."

Bunny nodded. "Arthur's room is the second on the left."

"I'll find it," said Billy.

Charley turned to Bunny. "Do you think your father will remember me?"

"Of course he will. We were best friends at school."

"We've both grown up a lot since then," said Charley, taking her police badge from her jacket pocket. She knocked on the door and, without waiting for an answer, opened it. "Detective Constable Charlotte Steel," she announced. "S.C.R.E.A.M. squad at your service."

Billy knew that no two crime scenes were the same. Some were gruesome. Some were mysterious. Some were just sad. He paused at the bottom of the stairs and braced himself for what he would discover in Arthur Smalbone's bedroom. Then, he placed one hand on the wooden rail and was surprised by the sudden sense of foreboding which struck him. It was like an icy waterfall and it left Billy chilled to the core. *What secrets are you hiding?* Billy wondered as he climbed the first step towards Arthur's bedroom. *What unwanted visitor has stolen all the peace from this house?*

Smallbone Manor was a sad place, Billy thought. Bunny had told them that her father hadn't wanted to keep the servants on after her mother had died. Billy was struck by the loneliness of it; just the major, Bunny and Arthur in this echoing house full of dusty half-used rooms and shadows. It was a million miles away from the two-up, two-down terrace that Billy had grown up in. Billy's home hadn't known a moment's peace. Five brothers, two sisters, Mum and Dad, one grandma, two grandpas and one extremely strange uncle, plus all the stolen goods that the rest of the Flint family could lay their thieving hands on, all meant that Billy's childhood certainly wasn't lonely. And the queue for the outside toilet was ridiculous.

Billy felt sorry for Bunny living here. Even with a younger brother to squabble with, a cook who apparently visited twice a day, and a housekeeper who came twice a week, it was too big. The empty eye sockets of a deer skull glared down at him from the wall. Too big and too creepy.

The stairs creaked and groaned as Billy climbed them, as if the house was protesting his presence. He reached the landing and headed for Arthur's room – *second on the left*, Bunny had said, but Billy didn't need directions – his sixth sense led him there, like a dog being yanked on its lead.

Billy walked slowly now. His breath was loud in his ears. He had investigated a lot of spooky old houses – they spoke to him in whispers. Stones had memories. Rooms held on to their secrets; moments captured in time, like flies in a web. He arrived at the door. He turned the handle.

And then it hit him.

Major Smallbone stared at Charley. *"Charlotte Steel?* Is it really you?"

"It's really me," said Charley.

"So the police are employing crippled girls now?" The words hung in the air like a bad smell. "What on earth do you think *you* can do to help?"

"She can rescue Arthur," said Bunny, with a hint of defiance.

Charley could see the vein on the side of the major's forehead pulse with emotion. "I'm sorry, Charlotte, but I don't see how you can help."

Charley softened. Major Smallbone was under incredible pressure. "My partner and I have unique experience in these sorts of cases."

"Missing persons cases?" said Major Smallbone.

"Missing persons who may have been kidnapped by –" Charley chose her words carefully – "something not human."

"Not human? What *are* you babbling about?" The major's temper was rising again.

"I have been successfully involved in numerous investigations where the solution was outside of the normal."

"What's all this?" Constable Dunstable spoke for the first time.

"Billy and I have just returned from Scotland where we investigated sightings of a sea monster in Loch Ness. The week before that we captured a thoroughly unpleasant creature called Old Tommy Rawhead that was terrorizing the little village of Oswaldstwistle in Lancashire. When the criminal turns out to be a zombie or a witch or a spectre, then, in my experience, the regular police are about as effective as a fish on a bicycle; no offence, Constable."

"Now listen 'ere," said Constable Dunstable. "We might not have your fancy-shmancy London ways here in Hobb's End, but we don't need no help from the likes of you. Major Smallbone has already explained the whole incident to me." Dunstable checked his notebook. "Young Archie—"

"Arthur," Charley corrected.

"– went to the carnival without permission and got a proper scolding, so he climbed out of 'is bedroom window and has run off somewhere." The constable closed his notepad as if that was the whole case solved.

"And I shall give him a damn good thrashing when he comes back!" snorted the major.

"Yes," said Bunny dryly, "that should teach him not to get kidnapped."

"And would you like Bunny to give you her eyewitness account of what *actually* happened?" Charley challenged.

"I saw something," Bunny began. "It had glowing red eyes and—"

"Just a silly girl's imagination," said Constable Dunstable. "Going to that carnival filled Miss Bunny's head up with all sorts of foolishness."

"I'm always telling Bunny off for her ridiculous imagination," said the major, as if that solved everything. "*I* don't have any imagination at all!"

"That I do believe," said Charley, under her breath. "It seems we will have to follow separate lines of enquiry, Constable Dunstable."

"I'd be glad if you did," said Dunstable irritably. "I've got a busy night. That young scallywag Fred Hawkins has gone an' lost himself too. I can't be hanging around here when I've got proper police work to do."

*Fred Hawkins*, Charley made a mental note.

Dunstable gave the major a quick salute and managed to poke himself in the eye.

"Fish on a bicycle," said Charley.

As Billy stepped over the threshold and into Arthur's room his skin began to crawl.

There were traces of the supernatural lingering on the air. They were faint, like the waft of tobacco two days after the cigarette has been smoked, but they were there nevertheless. Confirmation that whatever had taken Arthur Smallbone was not a man in disguise, but a monster.

The sensation started on the back of Billy's neck.

The hairs rose as if an unseen presence behind him had exhaled a cloud of frosty breath. The creeping terror spread over his scalp and then with a shudder it rippled down his spine; the stroke of an icy hand. Billy knew that beneath his clothes he was covered in pimply gooseflesh.

He didn't move. But his eyes scanned the room.

It was a boy's room, filled with a boy's things. Toy soldiers fighting a war on the bookshelf, marbles all over the floor, a half-eaten toffee apple still on the bedside table.

The bed where Arthur lay.

The window where the *creature* broke in.

The claw marks on the window sill.

Billy traced his fingers over the marks. They were deep gashes, made by large, sharp, powerful talons. Not natural. Not nice. They had to rescue Arthur, and quickly.

Billy headed back down the stairs in time to see Constable Dunstable leaving.

"Before you go," Billy called out to him, "did you examine the bedroom?"

"Course I did," said Dunstable. "I'm not the village idiot."

"So what did you make of the claw marks?"

"A cat, I reckon," said Dunstable. "Or p'raps a very large bird."

*Definitely not the village idiot*, Billy said to himself as Dunstable closed the front door behind him. *He hasn't got the brains.*

# CHAPTER FOUR

## COCONUTS OF DOOM

After Constable Dunstable had left, Major Smallbone marched into his study and slammed the door behind him.

"He's not happy about having you here," said Bunny.

"Your father will thank you when we've got your brother back," said Billy. "In the meantime, Charley and I are going to check out this carnival for ourselves. I want to retrace your steps."

"I thank you *now*," said Bunny, pushing a photograph of Arthur into Billy's hand. A cheeky boy grinned back at Billy, all freckles and sticky-out ears.

Charley and Billy left the house, each lost in their own thoughts. Night was drawing in. House lights glowed in the windows as the sky turned from blue to velvet black. The warmth of the day slipped away and Charley buttoned her jacket against the creeping chill. "I think we just have to follow the screams," she said with a laugh.

There was a constant stream of people heading towards the carnival and Charley and Billy joined the crowd. A poster had been pinned to a tree. It showed a man dressed as the Devil, complete with horns and a flowing red cape. Billy ripped the poster down and began to read aloud.

# ROLL UP. ROLL UP. IF YOU DARE.
## to DOCTOR VINDICTA'S CARNIVAL!

* Gasp at the dancing ghosts!
* Grimace at the creepy clowns!
* Giggle in the hall of mirrors!

## IT'S FRIGHTFULLY GOOD FUN!

Billy helped Charley as they crested a small hill. They saw a village of tents beneath them. The laughing and shrieking grew louder as they drew nearer.

"It does sound like fun," said Billy.

Charley nodded. "I can see why Bunny and Arthur sneaked out."

A steam organ piped up, adding to the noise. It was playing a dramatic tune, conjuring up emotions of mounting dread.

"It's 'The Dream of a Witches' Sabbath'," said Charley, recognizing the tune. "Composed by Berlioz."

"Cheerful chap is he, this Burly-O?" said Billy. "I prefer something you can sing along to." Billy cleared his throat and burst into song. *"Daddy wouldn't buy me a bow-wow! Bow-wow! I've got a little cat, and I'm very fond of that, but I'd rather have a bow-wow wow!"*

"That's quite enough of that, thank you." Charley gave Billy a playful thump, but they were both smiling.

A collection of brightly coloured tents and booths spread out across the common, made all the more magical in the lamplight. There was a Ferris wheel, a carousel, even a helter-skelter. Wisps of mist drifted across the ground as the last of the day's heat died, and Charley almost felt that her wheelchair could be a boat, parting a foamy sea. *Only boats aren't this much hard work*, she thought as she heaved herself onwards with her strong arms. Billy would have helped her again if she'd asked him to, but he knew her too well to offer.

"Are you picking anything up, Billy?"

"I can smell candyfloss."

"Is that a clue?"

"Nah," said Billy, "but I always get candyfloss at the fair. Do you think it would be wrong to eat on duty?"

"We haven't eaten since those awful sandwiches at the station when we changed trains," said Charley. "I'm starving. The first jacket potato seller we pass, the treat's on me."

"You're a gem," said Billy, his stomach growling. "Shall we get some pickled eggs too?"

Charley didn't answer that question. Instead she pointed at the hideous clown stumbling towards them through the fog.

The figure was tall. Taller than a normal human, with abnormal legs and a staggering gait. The clown's clothes were brightly coloured but ragged. A jagged slash of red gave it a hideous smile from ear to ear and long black tears smeared its cold, white cheeks. Clumps of green hair sprouted from a bald scalp.

"That has to be the worst wig I've seen in ages," chuckled Charley, as the stilt-walking clown wobbled by, making children squeal and laugh with delight before scattering them like startled pigeons.

"Remember that werewolf we met that was going bald?"

"How could I forget!" laughed Charley. "We trapped him when he was trying to rob the wig shop!"

"One wig stuck on his head and a chest wig glued on his back, poor thing."

Still laughing, they passed underneath a banner strung between two tent poles. It read in large letters,

# DR VINDICTA'S CARNIVAL OF MONSTERS.
## ENTER IF YOU DARE.

"We dare," said Charley, quite relieved that duckboards had been laid to provide pathways between the rows of attractions. She gave Billy the nod, and he bumped her wheelchair over the lip and onto the wooden planks where the going was much easier.

Charley and Billy worked their way through the crowd.

Charley never forgot that she was searching for clues about the lost boy and the monster that had taken him, but even she couldn't help being a little swept up by the heady atmosphere of thrills and chills. The carnival stallholders added another frightful element. Just like the stilt-walker, they were dressed as ghastly clowns with fearsome smiles and black-rimmed eyes. However, in their line of work Charley and Billy had come face-to-face with revenants – *real* walking corpses – and clowns, even scary ones, weren't in the same league.

The carousel was an especially sinister sight. Instead of the usual brightly painted wooden horses, on this ride the carved animals were all skeletons. There was something quite unsettling about seeing the young girls and boys smiling with glee, their arms flung tightly round the bony necks of the undead horses. Nevertheless, children bothered their parents for pennies and jostled each other as they queued excitedly for one attraction after another.

"The Helter-Skelter of Horror," Billy read as they approached the wooden tower. "What makes it so horrific, I wonder?" Then he saw the bats swooping in circles around it.

"Vampire bats?"

"Stuffed bats," observed Charley. "The wings don't flap. They must be on invisible strings or wires operated from inside the tower, I'd guess. But effective nevertheless."

There were all the usual stalls you might hope to find at a carnival too: a fortune teller, dressed as a witch; toffee apples, although they had been renamed "shrunken heads on sticks"; a hoopla game where, instead of throwing rope rings over tent pegs, you threw "fallen angel halos" over "coffin nails". Charley and Billy found the candyfloss seller, dressed as a vampire just as Bunny had said. The "vampire" was a small man with a shiny, bald head and a large set of uncomfortable-looking false teeth, complete with fangs and raspberry sauce on his lips for blood. He was sorry that he didn't remember talking to a girl of Bunny's description, and he was sorry again that he didn't recognize the photo of Arthur. "I see so many kids." He gave Billy some candyfloss, although at the Carnival of Monsters it was described as "dead man's hair". "Hope you find the young lad," he called after them.

"What a nice man," said Charley, as they left the candyfloss stall behind. "He'd starve to death if he was a *genuine* vampire."

The next attraction was the Coconut Shy of Doom, where each coconut had been painted to look like a skull.

"If I knock down three coconuts I win you a teddy bear," said Billy, handing Charley his candyfloss.

Before Charley could answer, Billy had paid the man and was taking aim. He didn't win a teddy, much to Charley's relief, but he did get a coconut, which he shoved into his satchel with a grin.

"What are you doing to do with that?" asked Charley.

Billy shrugged. "I might get hungry later."

"Do you think of anything except food?"

"I think of solving crimes," said Billy, "and I can't do that on an empty stomach. So, where to next? How about we try over there?"

Charley followed Billy's line of vision and pulled a disgusted face. The tent had a banner over the door which read: *The Human Horrors – Lizard Boy and Wolf Girl!*

"I don't think so," said Charley. "We'll either be forced to see some poor children suffering from a terrible skin condition and facial hair, or more unconvincing make-up. I've got Bunny's list of all the attractions she and Arthur went to, we'll check those out first."

Billy nodded. "The carnival might have nothing to do with Arthur's kidnapping at all, you know, it could just be a creepy coincidence. So the sooner we can rule it in or out, the better."

"I agree," said Charley. "But don't forget that Constable Dunstable mentioned *another* missing boy, Fred Hawkins. We also have to consider that this case is bigger than just Arthur Smallbone."

At that instant a deafening *BOOM!* echoed through the carnival. The ground actually shook beneath their feet. A great gasp of shock came up from the crowd, followed by the distinctive smell of gunpowder.

"An explosion!" said Charley, looking around for the source. "Large calibre cannon, by the sound of it."

"There!" said Billy, pointing up into the sky. A human figure was hurtling through the air wearing a cloak shaped like bat wings and a hood with pointy ears sewn on it. "I guess we've found the Amazing Man-Bat Bunny mentioned," he chuckled.

Charley traced the line of the man's trajectory back to the smoking barrel of a huge cannon. "A human cannonball," she said. "I think we can safely cross him off our list of suspects."

Billy grinned. "Yep, one thing we can count on is that whoever took Arthur, they didn't lug a blooming great cannon to their house and fire themselves up at his window."

There was a tremendous *oooohhhhhh* from the crowd as the daredevil landed safely in a net.

"You wouldn't catch me doing that for a hundred pounds," said Billy, as the "man-bat" staggered to his feet and took a bow.

"I didn't think you were scared of heights."

"It's not the height, it's the falling and the landing and the being smashed to pieces that puts me off."

"Fair point," said Charley.

Suddenly her face was one hundred per cent police officer again, her bright blue eyes as clear and sharp as diamonds. "There!" She pointed at a flash of red. "Tell me that you saw that too, Billy Flint."

Billy nodded. "Red skullcap, horns, red cape, forked tail, the same as on the posters. It *must* be Dr Vindicta himself. If anyone knows what's going on at the Carnival of Monsters, it'll be him. I've got some questions I'd like to ask."

"So have I," said Charley, "but let's save them for later. I think we should work our way through Bunny's list first. We'll follow in their footsteps and see what we can find but after that, Billy Flint, you and I have a date with the Devil."

## CHAPTER FIVE

# DOES MY BUM LOOK BIG IN THIS?

The first attraction which Bunny and Arthur had visited was the "Minotaur's Maze of Mirrors". There was a large queue lined up outside the marquee, but Billy walked straight to the front with Charley beside him, much to the annoyance of the crowd.

"Police!" said Charley, flashing her badge.

"Likely story," a pot-bellied man muttered, but he grudgingly moved aside anyway.

Billy lifted the entrance flap. A Minotaur was waiting for them inside.

It wasn't a real Minotaur, obviously. It was another

man in costume. A very big man. Naked to the waist and bulging with muscles. The full head-mask was pretty impressive, Charley thought. It really did look like a very savage bull – although close up Charley could see that one of the horns had been snapped off and then glued back on slightly wonky.

"We need to search your tent," said Billy.

The Minotaur didn't budge. He blocked their path and held out a meaty hand.

"Fo pen," said a muffled voice from inside the mask.

"I'm sorry?" said Charley.

"*Ah sa*, da ll be fo pen."

"Still not getting it," said Billy.

The Minotaur lifted his mask with a sigh. "I said, that'll be fourpence." He held his hand out for the money.

"That will be fourpence, *please*," said Charley.

The Minotaur sighed again. "That'll be fourpence, *please*."

"Much better," said Charley, wheeling right past the Minotaur without paying.

"Oi! What about the money? It's tuppence each for the maze."

"We're police," Charley called over her shoulder. "Send the bill to Scotland Yard!"

"I'm with her," said Billy, following his partner into the tent.

A second tent flap separated the entrance and the Minotaur guard from the attraction itself. Charley stopped in her tracks when she came face-to-face with her own reflection.

"Do I really look like that?" she asked Billy when he arrived beside her. They both stared into the mirror. Charley had a tiny body and a head like a balloon.

"Yes," said Billy. "Only in real life your head is slightly bigger."

They pushed on through the maze, doing their best as professional police officers not to be distracted by the ridiculous images they passed. However, it soon became clear that there was nothing to be found here, so rather than go back out the way they had come, they decided to race through the maze as fast as they could.

"Stumpy," said Billy, stealing a sideways glance at Charley's shrunken reflection in one mirror.

"Lanky," Charley retaliated, seeing Billy's impossibly stretched body in the next mirror.

"Lardy."

"Pinhead."

"Fat ar—"

"Leave it!" warned Charley.

They reached the end and emerged back into the night. "Where next?" said Billy.

"'The Ghost Dance'," said Charley. "Over there."

This time a clown with a rubber axe in his head met them at the entrance.

"Official business," said Charley, showing her police badge. The clown shrugged. "Do you remember talking to this boy?" she asked, holding up the picture of Arthur Smallbone.

The clown squinted. "No," he said. "Should I?"

"He's missing," said Billy. "And he came here on the night he disappeared."

"Can't help you," said the clown. "Sorry."

"Another dead end," whispered Charley as they moved away. "Shall we just move on down Bunny's list?"

"Maybe wait for a minute," suggested Billy, "see the first part of the act. There's something fishy about this carnival, I'm convinced of it. We just haven't found it yet."

The marquee had a large stage area at one end, hidden for now behind black velvet curtains. Charley and Billy positioned themselves to one side of the audience, so they could both get a view of the stage, and make a quick exit if they needed to. In front of the curtains, the limelights burned brightly, their sickly yellow glow adding to the ghostly scene.

"Do you think that clown was trying to hide something?" said Charley. She was getting frustrated by their lack of progress.

"You never can tell," said Billy. "People get funny when you show them a police badge. My grannie always does."

"Your grannie is a bank robber," said Charley.

"Fair point," said Billy. His ears pricked up. "Can you hear something hissing?"

"It's the limelights," Charley explained. "Under that stage there'll be canisters of oxygen and hydrogen. The gases whoosh down separate pipes under pressure, then they come together and they're lit. They make a brilliant flame that's directed at a cylinder of 'quicklime'. It's actually calcium oxide and it can be heated up to 4,662° Fahrenheit. That's how those really bright stage lights are produced."

Billy gave her a toothy smile. "How do you fit so much knowledge in your head?"

"I read books," said Charley. She was about to say something more when the hubbub in the tent dropped and a figure walked out onstage.

"Look, Ma! A skellington!" yelled a boy in the front row.

To be fair to the lad it did look like a skeleton. Well, a bit, anyway. It was a man wearing a black suit and face mask, onto which the bones of the human body had been painted. Charley had more than a passing knowledge of anatomy and this skeleton was pretty basic. But, even so, in the flickering light the effect was chilling.

"Ladies and gentlemen, boys and girls," the skeleton addressed the crowd. "Welcome to our story of sorrow, a story that will you chill you to the marrow..." The audience listened in hushed silence. At the skeleton's signal the curtains were drawn back to reveal the scene. A cobweb-covered chandelier hung from the ceiling, and a wilting bouquet of roses sat in the middle of a dining table, set with two empty chairs. "There was once a woman named Gloria," said the skeleton, and as he spoke a ghostly figure materialized on the stage. The crowd gasped. "And she was in love with a man named Basil. They were going to be married one day...but their love was doomed!"

"I think I've wet myself, Ma," said the boy in the front row.

Charley did not wet herself, but she did stare in fascination. The ghostly woman had long blonde hair, as white as ash. Her pale lips were moving, but no sound came out. Her expression was full of grief, made all the more intense by the tatty wedding dress she wore. Charley could see straight through her; the table, the chairs, everything.

The skeleton continued his tale. "Her fiancé never returned from the war...except as a phantasm. And every night they dance in death the wedding dance they never performed in life!"

A second ghost appeared onstage, a man dressed in a top hat and black suit...the groom. He reached for his bride's hand. From somewhere offstage an out-of-tune piano began to play and the two ghosts danced beneath the chandelier, the table and chairs passing through their disembodied forms.

"Come on," whispered the little boy's mum. "I'm about to wet myself too."

"All very impressive," Charley whispered. "But there's a very rational explanation. The real dancers are offstage behind the curtain. They're being reflected by a carefully positioned sheet of glass on the other side of the stage. It's still a good illusion though."

The crowd started to mutter. Someone threw their toffee apple at the stage and it slammed into the wall of glass and stuck there, suspended in the air. "She's right," said one man. "It's all a bloomin' con!"

The skeleton glared at Charley. At least she felt like it was glaring.

"Let's go," said Billy. "We won't learn anything more here."

Charley didn't argue. "It's quite a famous stage trick actually," she explained as they left the tent. "It's called 'Pepper's Ghost' after John Henry Pepper, the man who invented it. Quite impressive, wasn't it?"

"Yes," said Billy, "unless you've seen real ghosts."

"Like we have," said Charley. She looked at Bunny's list and sighed. "One more to go," she said. "The Wheel of the Devil. Fingers crossed we turn up something there, otherwise we're no closer to finding Arthur."

In the deepening darkness the make-up on the stallholders was more effective, the scares seemed scarier, the excitement more intense. The carnival was still thronging with people with no sign of letting up. The steam-powered rides spun and whirled in dizzying circles, the organ was piping another eerie tune. A strongman dressed as Frankenstein's monster was challenging a young man to test his strength.

"Sorry to bother you," said Charley. "Could you direct us to the Wheel of the Devil?"

The monster pointed to another marquee.

Charley and Billy queue-jumped again. Billy hesitated. The hairs on the back of his hand were starting to rise. "I've got a bad feeling about this tent."

"Excellent," said Charley, brightening up. "That's the best news I've had all night!"

# CHAPTER SIX

# WHEEL OF THE DEVIL

Billy's "bad feeling" meant that they were probably about to encounter something supernatural, which, hopefully, would bring them closer to Arthur Smallbone. "How do you want to play this?" whispered Billy as they drew closer. "I'm guessing that matey there dressed as the Devil is Dr Vindicta, judging from the posters anyway. Should we show him our badges and let him know we want a word with him?"

"I don't think so," said Charley, stroking her chin. "I'd like the chance to observe Dr Vindicta *before* he knows that we're police."

"Very cunning, Duchess."

The queue flowed steadily into the marquee. Charley and Billy paid their money this time, so as not to draw attention to themselves, and merged with the crowd. They took in their surroundings in the way that only trained detectives can, looking for *details*, the tiny things which they knew could solve a case if they pieced them all together.

The tent was huge, with two poles supporting the roof. Between those two poles was a circular arena. In the middle of the arena sat an enormous cylinder – the wheel – and the public gathered around that arena, standing in a circle. Charley and Billy were able to find themselves a space at the front with a perfect view of both the wheel itself and Dr Vindicta.

Up close, Dr Vindicta's disguise was shabby rather than sinister. The red cloak was fading, the scarlet skullcap with horns had a sweat stain around the rim. The waxed moustache and forked beard were probably dyed black. But the fierce eyes were real enough. "Prepare to be amazed!" growled Dr Vindicta, his black eyes glaring out above his hollow cheeks. "Prepare to be terrified!" Small flecks of hot spit escaped Vindicta's lips.

Billy nudged Charley. "He's really working himself up, isn't he?"

"All carnival callers have to get the crowd going, but Dr Vindicta is taking this very seriously." Charley paused. "He almost seems desperate, as if he *needs* us to be afraid."

"There's nothing supernatural about Dr Vindicta," said Billy. "But I can't shake the feeling that something paranormal is lurking in this tent."

"I don't think it's the 'wheel' though. I've seen these devices before, although not on such a large scale," said Charley. "It's science, not magic."

The "Wheel of the Devil" filled the middle of the tent. It appeared to be made of paper with a wooden and metal frame, and it was carefully balanced on a merry-go-round so that it could spin freely. There were vertical slits evenly spaced around the outside of the blank wheel, like windows. Billy couldn't fathom out how it worked. "What am I looking at?"

"It's called a zoetrope," said Charley, as if that explained everything.

"And where does the Grim Reaper come in?" asked Billy, indicating the motionless figure of a hooded skeleton standing between Dr Vindicta and the zoetrope.

"I was wondering that myself," said Charley. The model skeleton was a chilling sight. The skull beneath the hood was made of metal, not bone, but it was frighteningly realistic. Charley could easily imagine the eyeless sockets staring straight at her.

"I think we're about to find out," said Charley as the tent flaps closed and the audience fell silent.

"I am Dr Vindicta," declared the showman. "Welcome to my world of wicked wonders! Gaze on the ghastly ghoulishness! Shudder at the sinister shadows! Marvel at the malicious mime! Allow me to demonstrate the devilish delights of...*the Wheel of the Devil!*"

Using his red cape like a curtain to hide his movements, Dr Vindicta did *something* to the metal skeleton and then stood back. With a whir and a click, the skeleton stirred into life. The head looked left, then right, scanning the audience, the metal teeth in its metal jaw clacking together.

"Did you see what Vindicta did?" said Billy.

"No," hissed Charley. "Keep watching."

The skeleton was holding a winch in its metal fingers, with the sort of sturdy handle which might otherwise have brought a bucket up from the bottom of a deep well. Now the skeleton started to turn the handle, slowly at first but getting faster and faster. And in response the zoetrope began to spin…

All eyes were on the revolving wheel. As it spun Billy could see a picture *through* the vertical slits…and the picture was moving. It was the silhouette of a boy and as the zoetrope spun the boy performed a series of cartwheels, tumbling like an acrobat.

"It's another illusion," said Charley under her breath. "A simple scientific trick which fools your eyes. It works by persistence of vision. You see a series of static pictures whizzing by so quickly that your brain fills in the gaps. I had one of these at home, actually, only much, much smaller. It came with a collection of paper slides – each one showed a series of pictures with small variations: a horse jumping a fence, a fox running from a hound, that sort of thing. Its name, zoetrope, comes from the Greek – 'zoe' meaning 'life' and 'tropos' which means 'turning'. So it is, literally, a wheel of life."

"All very interesting, but it's not very scary, is it?" said Billy.

The wheel came to a halt. The silhouette boy froze mid tumble. "And now," roared Dr Vindicta, "the second spin. Hang on to your sanity."

"Let's go," said Charley. "Unless you change the

wheel, the images are exactly the same *every* time. That's how a zoetrope works."

Charley spun her chair around but Billy stopped her. "Not this time, Duchess."

Billy watched with mounting surprise. The silhouette boy was just the same. Same mop of hair, same shorts, same knobbly knees. But this time he didn't cartwheel. This time he produced some balls from his pocket and began to juggle them.

Billy's skin was stinging; the presence of the supernatural was so powerful. And growing by the moment.

All of the crowd were spellbound, unable to believe their eyes…

The boy threw the balls into the air and dropped them.

Although he was just an image, the boy seemed scared and his fear spread through the tent. Billy's own head was starting to spin…

The boy picked up the balls. And fumbled again.

Billy's whole body was prickling now, every inch of his skin was screaming. *Something wicked is coming.* "We need to get out," he hissed to Charley. But Charley was mesmerized, unable to drag her eyes away.

The boy stooped for the balls a third time but he didn't reach them. A dog had joined him. A massive dog with slavering jaws, lips drawn back to reveal dagger-like teeth.

The boy ran. The dog ran. It was not a fair race. The boy was going to lose.

The whole tent was filled with fear. One woman fainted. Dr Vindicta clapped his hands gleefully like a spiteful schoolboy. Billy needed to get out of the tent – out of the overwhelming presence of evil. He staggered and stumbled towards the exit, with Charley half supporting his weight with her chair, until he fell out of the tent and into the cold night air.

Behind them the audience was now screaming, but two voices rose above the madness. Glancing back they saw a little girl sobbing, "That's my friend, Fred." And Dr Vindicta, laughing like a madman.

# CHAPTER SEVEN

# As Slippery as an Eel

Outside the tent, Billy was gasping for breath as if his head had been held underwater for too long. Trembling, he looked at his hands; the stinging was fading as the power of the zoetrope subsided, but his mind was still spinning as he tried to understand what had just happened.

"The girl!" said Charley.

Billy looked at Charley, confused and groggy. "What girl?"

"The girl who said she recognized the boy in the wheel," said Charley. "We have to talk to her! Where did she go?"

"What about Dr Vindicta?"

"We know where to find him," answered Charley. "But if we lose that girl, we've lost her for ever. She said the shadow figure was Fred – she might just be talking about the *other* missing boy: Fred Hawkins."

Charley's crisp words were the slap in the face that Billy needed to bring him completely to his senses. "Small," he said, trying to picture the girl he had barely noticed. "Slight build, patch on her dress…"

Billy scanned the crowd as it scattered in all directions, dispersing back into the carnival. He couldn't see her.

"Tartan ribbon, dark hair…" Charley continued the description, her eyes seeking the girl out too. "*There!*"

"Hey!" Billy called. "Can we have a word with you?"

The girl turned, saw Billy…and fled, weaving through the sea of people as quickly as an eel. Billy gave chase, but the crowds were packed together, and he lost precious seconds saying "Sorry" and "'Scuse me" and "Can I come through?" while the girl was getting away.

Outside of the tent and away from the influence of the wicked zoetrope, the crowd were more confused than afraid, as if they had woken up from a bad dream. They had stopped screaming and were now looking for another delicious thrill to try at Dr Vindicta's Carnival of Monsters. With just a little bit more pushing and shoving Billy finally broke through the pack and out the other side. He looked all around, but to his annoyance it seemed that the girl had managed to give him the slip.

"Where are you?" he murmured.

He was about to give up and go back to Charley when he caught a glimpse of a dark-haired girl with a tartan ribbon up ahead. The girl was standing behind a man – her father, Billy guessed. But he realized he was wrong when he saw the girl skilfully and carefully ease her slender hand into the man's jacket pocket, take out his wallet and then run away again!

Billy wasn't about to let her get away a second time. He ran round behind one of the carnival tents and emerged right in the little thief's path. The girl didn't have time to stop. She ran right into Billy.

"Police," said Billy. "I want a word with you."

The girl looked around wildly as if she was going to dash for it again, but Billy placed a hand on her shoulder. "Don't even try," he said.

The girl slumped, defeated…and then kicked Billy on the shins. Really hard. Billy let go and the girl laughed and ran again. Only to find her escape route cut off by Charley Steel. It was the pickpocket's turn to be surprised and before she could react, Charley had whipped out her handcuffs and chained the girl's wrist to the arm of her wheelchair. "You aren't going anywhere, young lady."

This time the girl knew that she had met her match and she stood there looking sorry for herself. "I only took one wallet, honest," she sniffed, wiping a trail of snot on the cuff of her dress. "And these two watches," she went on, emptying her pockets onto Charley's lap. "And this pen. Oh and these other watches. An' that's it."

"I'm not interested in the thefts," said Billy. "So long as you hand over that swag so it can be returned."

The girl nodded with some relief. "What sort of police are you then?"

"The scary kind," said Charley.

"We need to talk to you," said Billy, ushering the girl away from the crowd and beyond prying ears. "I'm Billy," he said. "What's your name?"

"Newt," she said. "Newt Frogget."

"Well then, Newt Newt Frogget," said Billy, "back in Dr Vindicta's tent you called out a boy's name when you were watching the zoetrope. Why did you do that?"

"Because it was Fred," said Newt.

"What was?"

"The shadow, the boy in the wheel, it was Fred Hawkins."

"Fred Hawkins," Charley repeated, with a knowing look at Billy.

"You mean the silhouette *looked* like Fred?" said Billy.

"Yeah," said Newt. "Same pointy-up nose, same haircut, same everything."

"But it was only a silhouette," said Billy.

"It's Fred," said Newt, a small tear pooling in her eye. "I'd know him anywhere. We often go out pickpock— Er – *playing* together."

Charley raised her eyebrows. "We need you to take us to Fred's house."

"But it's late," Newt protested. "Past my bedtime."

"Either you take us to Fred's house, or we take you to see Constable Dunstable."

"It's this way!" said Newt quickly.

"That was a sudden change of mind," said Charley with a smile.

Billy walked a pace behind the two girls. His goosebumps had disappeared, but the nagging sense of danger remained, like spiders scuttling back and forth across his brain. All that he could think about was the silhouette of the monstrous dog chasing the silhouette

71

which looked like Fred Hawkins. One question hammered loudly in Billy's mind... *What the Hell was happening in Hobb's End?*

## CHAPTER EIGHT

# A Dangerous Game

"That's Fred's house," said Newt as they turned the corner into a run-down terrace.

"Thank you," said Charley, unlocking the handcuffs and fulfilling her part of the bargain. Newt disappeared into the night with a skip in her step.

On instinct, Charley checked Newt's stash of stolen goods, which she had packed into her satchel for safekeeping. "She's taken the wallet again," she sighed.

The Hawkins house was a family home. The windows were smeared with child-sized handprints, the front wall was scrawled with chalk. The tiny garden was littered with one-armed dolls and a wonky-wheeled bike. From inside Charley could hear lots of children. Playing, yelling, squabbling.

Billy knocked loudly on the front door. There was a brief lull in the noise from inside the house, but the door remained stubbornly shut.

"Police," said Billy, raising his voice.

Five long seconds passed and Billy was about to knock again when the door opened a crack. A tired woman peered out. She had a baby in her arms that was no more than a few months old, Charley guessed, and a toddler with a snotty nose wrapped around her legs. Both children were crying. Behind them Charley could see five more little ones jumping on the battered furniture. The woman looked as if *she* might start crying soon.

"Detective Constables William Flint and Charlotte Steel," said Billy, flashing his police badge. "S.C.R.E.A.M. squad."

"Is this about my Fred?" she asked. "'Ave you found him?" The words caught in her throat as if she was expecting the worst. "Constable Dunstable said 'e was getting some men together to search the woods."

"No," said Billy, "he hasn't been found yet."

"But we do have a clue as to his whereabouts," added Charley. "We just need to ask you a few questions."

"You'd best come in," said Mrs Hawkins. She looked embarrassed by the chaos of her home and the children running wild. "I've told 'em to git to bed, but they won't go." Mrs Hawkins visibly sagged, as if all the air had gone out of her.

"Bed!" snapped Charley, showing her police badge to the children. "Now! Or I'll arrest you on a section 96B!"

The three boys and two girls took one look at Charley's face, saw that she wasn't kidding, and shot up the stairs, leaving Mrs Hawkins with her two little ones.

"Thank you," she said, slumping into a battered chair with relief, still clutching her baby and toddler. "What is a section 96B?"

"It's a serious offence," Charley explained warmly. "Driving your mother mad."

Mrs Hawkins's lips made a tired smile but it didn't reach the woman's eyes. "So, you two helpin' Constable Dunstable find my Fred, then? You said you had a clue?"

"We don't know for sure," admitted Billy, "but we think that the Carnival of Monsters might have something to do with it."

"His pa told 'im not to go," said Mrs Hawkins. She sighed. "Don't s'pose Fred paid a blind bit of notice though."

"When was the last time you saw Fred?" asked Charley, her voice so soft it was almost a whisper.

"Breakfast yesterday. I did 'im a lovely bowl of porridge and he gobbled it up," she said with a mother's pride. "I hope he's eaten something, wherever he is."

"Do you have any idea where he might have gone after that porridge? From what you've said I'm guessing he bunked off school and went to the carnival."

Mrs Hawkins's lip began to quiver.

"We know this isn't easy for you," Charley said reassuringly, "just a couple more questions and then we'll get going."

The two smallest children had dropped off to sleep, one cradled in each of Mrs Hawkins's arms. Mrs Hawkins snuggled them against her, taking comfort in their snores and the heat of their breath. She nodded. "If it will help get Fred back."

"When did you first realize that Fred was missing?" asked Billy.

"When he didn't come home for 'is tea," said Mrs Hawkins. "I wasn't worried for the first hour or so, like.

Fred often goes wondering with Newt Frogget, getting into all sorts of mischief, I shouldn't wonder."

Charley knew this wasn't the time to break the news that Fred was a thief in training. For now he was a missing boy, and that was all that mattered. "So what did you do?"

"Me and Mr H looked in all the usual places where Fred likes to play. He goes fishin' and he's got a den in the woods...we looked until it was too dark to look no more. Then we went to see Constable Dunstable."

"And your husband, Mr Hawkins, is he still out looking for Fred now?" Charley glanced at her watch; it was nearly midnight.

Mrs Hawkins shook her head. "It's a Friday," she explained, "and Friday is Chess Club."

"Your husband must take it very seriously, to be out so late, and at a time like this."

"It's his only night off all week, so I can't complain," said Mrs Hawkins. "My husband works hard, and Chess Club is his way of unwinding. I don't know how much actual chess gets played, mind. I think there's some drinking and some card playing too. Jim hasn't missed a meeting since his school days."

Charley arched her eyebrow quizzically, filing that

information away inside her brain, in a drawer marked *Odd things that people do.*

"Which school did your husband go to, if you don't mind me asking?"

"Milverton Hall," said Mrs Hawkins. "Jim was a scholarship boy. Did well to mix with all those posh lads." She looked around at their modest home. "Much good that it did him."

"You've been so helpful," Charley said, bringing the conversation to a close. "We must be going now, but if you think of anything else, please let us know. We're staying up at Major Smallbone's house."

They were at the door when Mrs Hawkins stopped them and thrust a photograph into Charley's hand. "My Fred," she said, "handsome, ain't he?"

The chubby baby in the picture had dark curly hair and was wearing a dress. Charley couldn't tell whether it was a boy or a girl. "Erm, thanks," said Charley, pocketing the picture, although she didn't know what possible use it might be. "How old is Fred, actually?"

"He's eleven," said Mrs Hawkins, "but that's the only photograph I've got."

The front door closed quietly behind them and Charley and Billy waited until they were up the garden path and out of earshot before they shared their thoughts.

"Do you think the two disappearances are linked?" asked Billy. "Could we have two missing boys on our hands instead of one?"

"It looks that way to me," said Charley, "although the only link we have is the carnival and I'm still no closer to knowing what on earth is going on there."

"I do know that something is very wrong in Hobb's End," said Billy. "You can feel it too, can't you, Charley? The fear."

Charley nodded.

"The Smallbones are afraid. The Hawkins family are afraid. But if word gets out that boys are going missing then this whole town might start to panic. Fear spreads faster than a cold."

A church bell sounded twelve deep chimes and then silence fell over Hobb's End. Lost in their own thoughts Charley and Billy made their way back to Bunny's house. Curtains were drawn, only a few lights were still burning. A stray dog wandered the street looking for lamp posts to wee against and perhaps another dog's bottom to sniff. The dog saw Charley and Billy and watched them cautiously, following at a distance. In the woods an owl hooted. Apart from that, Hobb's End was as silent as a graveyard. It was an eerie quiet, as if the town was holding its breath. *I don't like it*, thought Charley.

At that moment a sound echoed over the town – a deep and terrible howl.

Billy and Charley halted. "What was *that*?"

Somewhere in the distance a baby started to cry. The stray dog ran off with its tail between its legs, whimpering with fright. In the nearby woods a hundred crows took flight, squawking out their own terror as the spine-tingling howl trailed away.

"A wolf?" asked Billy, already knowing the answer.

"There aren't any wolves in England," said Charley.

"Some people think that there aren't any demons, either."

One more long and angry howl sounded through Hobb's End and then the deathly silence returned. Billy reached out for Charley's hand and clenched it tightly.

"We can stop it, partner," said Charley confidently. "Whatever *it* is."

# CHAPTER NINE

## ENDLESS NIGHT

Charley and Billy made the rest of the journey to Bunny's house in silence. For now, the trail was cold, and so were they. They let themselves in at the back door as suggested by the major, who had rather grudgingly agreed to host the two detectives. He considered their theories to be "balderdash" and "piffle", but nevertheless, he had turned his study into a makeshift bedroom for Charley, with a foldout bed and a table for her books, papers, and the microscope and chemistry set which she always brought with her on a case. Billy's room was upstairs but he wasn't ready for bed yet.

"Right, Duchess," said Billy, clapping his hands together. "I'll head for the kitchen and rustle up some supper, you stoke the fire and we can get cracking."

The flames were dying in the grate and Charley wheeled over and added another shovelful of coal. She tugged her blanket across her knees and went to the table, turning up the wick on the oil lamp so it glowed more brightly. It would be a long night.

Billy returned minutes later with a heavily laden tray.

"Tea," said Charley gleefully. She opened the lid of the pot and took a sniff. "Earl Grey; lovely."

"And I've got some bread we can toast on the fire. Some butter, potted meat, jam and cheese."

Charley picked up one of the slices of bread. It was about an inch thick. "Not very ladylike," she said.

"You're not a lady," Billy grinned. "You're a copper."

Billy took a toasting fork from its hook beside the fireplace and held the bread above the embers until it turned deep brown, almost charred around the edges. Holding it with his fingertips Billy tugged the bread from the fork, slathered it with butter and sliced it in half. "Jam, cheese or potted meat?"

"Just butter will be fine, thank you," she said.

Billy added a hunk of cheese to his toast, and then

put some more bread on the toasting fork with eager anticipation of a second slice. "So, Detective Constable Charlotte Steel," he said, with a small shower of crumbs. "Let's compare notes."

Charley opened her notepad. She wrote three headings and drew a large question mark above each. *Victims. Suspects. Clues.*

"So we're agreed there seem to be *two* victims," said Charley. "Arthur Smallbone *and* Fred Hawkins."

"Agreed," said Billy. "Two victims, *so far.*"

"Then we have the question of the Carnival of Monsters," said Charley. "I wondered at first whether it was pure coincidence that the kidnappings started when the carnival arrived in Hobb's End. It's an easy option to start blaming strangers when a crime happens in a small town, especially when the strangers are so...*strange.* But from what we witnessed with the zoetrope, we have to consider the possibility that there's a link."

Billy licked melted butter from his fingers. "I still want to talk to Dr Vindicta, there's definitely something fishy about him." He put another slab of bread on the toasting fork and thrust it over the glowing embers. "And I have to give the Wheel of the Devil a close examination, although I'd rather do that in daylight, given the choice."

"Are you scared, Billy?" It was a question between friends, not a taunt.

"Yes," said Billy quickly. Then, "No. Perhaps 'scared' is the wrong word." His brow furrowed. "I'm concerned that we've only scraped the tip of the iceberg, and that this case is turning into something bigger and more dangerous than we imagined."

"We didn't imagine that howl, did we?"

"No, we didn't," said Billy.

"Could there be a *real* monster at the Carnival of Monsters?" Charley wondered out loud, rattling her pencil between her teeth in annoyance. "And if there is, then where is it hiding?"

"The only trace of the supernatural I detected was that creepy zoetrope."

"So how do all these elements fit together? It's like trying to do a jigsaw puzzle when we don't know how many pieces there are and we don't even have a picture to give us a clue." The cogs of Charley's mind were spinning so fast now, Billy could almost hear them whirring. "Were Arthur and Fred taken at random? Or were they chosen for some special reason? If so, what reason? Is there some connection between the kidnapped boys? And if so, what is it?"

"I've been starting to wonder if the Hobb-Hound is real after all," said Billy. "I thought it was just another local legend at first, but I'm not so sure now. 'Boys being taken in the night' – wasn't that part of the poem?"

"*'So when the sun comes out to play, all the boys have gone away, Taken swiftly in the night, when the Hobb-Hound takes to flight!'*" quoted Charley. "But if the Hobb-Hound is real, why has it come back now?"

"And how is a *local* demon linked to a *travelling* funfair?"

"Argghh!" Charley snarled with frustration, biting through the end of her pencil. "So many questions!"

"Part of me wants to close the whole carnival down just to be on the safe side," said Billy. "Question everyone, take the apparatus apart bolt by bolt if we have to."

Charley shook her head. "It still might be nothing more than a coincidence."

"I don't believe that, and neither do you—" Billy's thoughts were interrupted by an unexpected noise. It was the unmistakable sound of a key turning in a lock. As they listened they heard the front door open with a creak and someone walk boldly inside. The footsteps were heavy, a man not a child, and they had the confident stride of a soldier.

"Major Smallbone?" Billy mouthed.

Charley checked her watch. Two thirty-seven in the morning. "Where's he been?" she mouthed back.

"Out looking for Arthur?" suggested Billy.

The footsteps stomped up the stairs and a bedroom door was firmly shut.

Now that her attention was focused inside the house, Charley could make out a second set of footsteps coming from the room above. "Do you hear that?" They were lighter than the major's and they moved restlessly, back and forth. Five steps forwards. Stop. Turn. Five steps back. Bunny was pacing.

"She's coming down," said Billy as the staircase squeaked.

Billy opened the study door. Bunny halted guiltily halfway down the stairs. "I'm sorry," Bunny said. "I thought everyone was in bed."

"Crime doesn't sleep, so neither do we," said Billy. "Well, not much anyway. Come and sit with us."

Gratefully, Bunny joined them. "I heard the awful howling at midnight, and what with that and Arthur, I wasn't able to get back to sleep…" Bunny pressed her fist against her lips as if she could hold back all the fear bottled up inside. For a moment it looked as if she had composed herself, but then her legs wobbled and she had to grab the table to stop herself from falling. "Oh, Charley, I'm so afraid that I'm going to lose my brother for ever."

"No, you're not, I promise we will get Arthur back," said Charley, moving across to comfort her friend. "Billy was just going to do some research, weren't you, Billy? And Bunny, you're going to sit with me by the fire."

Charley flicked her head towards the door and Billy took the hint. "Yeah, I want to work through the files that Luther gave us, so I'll say 'goodnight', ladies." He shut the door behind him, leaving the girls to it.

Bunny was trembling as she sat beside Charley in the half-light. "I'm so afraid," she said. "Arthur is annoying all day, every day, but he's the only brother I've got." She sank a little lower. "It's all my fault that the monster took him."

"Don't be ridiculous, Bunny. All you did was take your brother to the carnival for fun. You mustn't blame yourself."

Bunny nodded, but didn't look convinced. They slipped into silence then, gazing deeply into the fire, letting the crackling of the logs and the dancing flames bring their own special sense of peace.

"Do you remember our midnight feasts when we were at school?" said Bunny eventually, changing to a happier subject.

"And the biscuits we stole from matron?" Charley laughed.

"Yes, I'd forgotten that!" said Bunny, brightening up. "She was furious when she found out."

"Not as much as when you put that hedgehog in her bed."

"That was *you*, Charley Steel," Bunny laughed. "I remember the summer hols too, when you let me come and stay with you. All those lovely long walks we took with your dog. What was her name?" Bunny faltered awkwardly when she realized what she had said. Her eyes flicked to Charley's wheelchair and then flicked away just as quickly. "I'm sorry, I didn't mean to…"

Charley didn't miss a beat. "Her name was Dynamite. Such a beautiful Border collie."

"The most gorgeous brown eyes," said Bunny fondly.

"Happy days," said Charley.

Her old school chum looked impossibly sad at that moment; as little and lost as a boarder on her first night away from home.

"Don't give up hope, Bunny Smallbone." Charley

spoke with the compassion of a friend and the authority of a police officer. "Look at me."

"But that monster—"

"Will regret the day it ever took Arthur," said Charley. "This is what S.C.R.E.A.M. do, Bunny. We get to the bottom of mysteries like this and put a stop to them. Just in the last few weeks, Billy and I rounded up a whole flock of fairies in Cottingley. Spiteful little creatures." She showed Bunny the tip of her finger which was circled with fresh scar tissue. "Nearly bit the top of my finger right off. I'm not pretending that it's going to be easy, Bunny, but S.C.R.E.A.M. have solved every case and we don't intend to fail now."

Bunny was reassured by Charley's confidence and, pulling a blanket around herself, she curled up in the armchair by the fire and shut her eyes. "You always were my best friend, Charley."

"I hope you still think that by the end of the week," Charley whispered, returning to her books.


At some point Billy had come back down and they had all fallen asleep. Bunny in the armchair, Billy sprawled on the sofa, and Charley in her wheelchair, her forehead on the table in front of her. The fire was dead. The room had the cold, damp feel of early dawn. Charley heard footsteps outside the house and lifted her head with a groan.

The footsteps halted at the front door and were followed by a loud knock which echoed through the house. Charley felt the heaviness of that sound deep inside her; it wasn't the knock of a postman or a friendly neighbour. This knock was urgent.

"Duty calls, Billy Flint," said Charley, quickly tidying her long ginger hair and retying her ribbon as she went into the entrance hall. She reached the door at the same moment that Major Smallbone appeared at the top of the stairs, bleary eyed and wrapped in a dressing gown. The knock came again.

Charley found Constable Dunstable standing on the doorstep. The man had aged since they last met, or so it seemed. There was a look of desperation on his face. Dunstable was unshaven and two dark rims circled his eyes. His boots and uniform were mud splattered.

"Constable," said Charley, her feelings towards her fellow officer softening. "You look done in. Come in. Let me get you a cup of tea."

"I can't rest yet, but thank you anyway, Miss Steel."

He removed his helmet and pushed his hand through his bedraggled hair. "I just wanted the major here to know that we've been searching for young Arthur and Fred Hawkins through the night..."

"And?" said the major. Bunny and Billy were both in the hallway too now, waiting on a knife's edge.

"And we didn't find them I'm afraid." Constable Dunstable turned his head and looked away towards the woods. "We're going to keep lookin', of course. Try a bit further afield today..."

"There's something else, isn't there?" said Billy.

"Another boy went missing last night," he said wearily. "That makes three now."

# CHAPTER TEN

## TAKEN IN THE NIGHT

Constable Dunstable left in a hurry. Charley insisted that he have a cup of tea first, but she couldn't make him sit down and he drank it standing up in the hall. *No*, he didn't know of any link between the missing boys. *No*, he didn't think they had been taken against their will. *No*, he didn't think the howling last night was anything other than a dog. *No*, he didn't know what else to do except keep on searching.

Major Smallbone and Bunny left with him to help with the hunt. The major looked as if he had slept in his shirt, Charley noticed; it was creased and sweat-stained.

A pair of gold cufflinks flashed as he shoved his arms into his coat. She only caught a glimpse and she might have been mistaken but the cufflinks looked exactly like chess pieces – kings.

*Chess. Was Major Smallbone also a member of the mysterious Chess Club, the same as Fred Hawkins's father?* Charley wondered. That might explain why the major hadn't come home till the early hours of the morning. Another piece of the jigsaw puzzle? But where did it fit?

After a quick breakfast of boiled eggs and soldiers, Charley and Billy set out to follow their own chain of investigation. Constable Dunstable had given them the name of the third missing boy, along with his family's address and directions for how to get there.

Charley and Billy found the house easily enough. It was enormous.

"Nice gaff," said Billy, whistling between his teeth. "It's a good job my cousins aren't here or this would be going on their 'to do' list."

"'To do' list?"

"To burgle," said Billy. "This sort of house would be like Christmas and birthdays rolled into one for them."

They approached the black front door, the brass lion of the door knocker grinning back at them. "I suspect they would rather have lost every silver candlestick and gold necklace they possess," said Charley, "rather than have their son stolen from them in the middle of the night."

The door opened before they reached it and a butler stood aside for a small plump woman. "Have you found him?" she said. "Have you found Herbert?"

"I'm sorry, Mrs..." Charley quickly checked her notebook. "Fraser." Charley flashed her badge. "We just have a few questions that we need to ask you."

Mrs Fraser's shoulders slumped. "You'd best come in."

"Would you mind if I had a look around?" asked Billy. Mrs Fraser nodded wearily and while Billy headed upstairs, she led Charley into the front room. A man was standing by the window, looking out, his back to them.

"Mr Fraser?" said Charley.

The man turned. While Mrs Fraser was round and cuddly, Mr Fraser was the opposite. He was tall and thin, with bony elbows and jutting cheekbones above hollow cheeks. He was standing still, almost rooted to the spot, his fingers fidgeting constantly, quaking with worry. Nervously, Mr Fraser adjusted his tie. Charley instantly spotted his silver tiepin; it was in the shape of a castle.

A rook? *Another* chess piece? Charley filed that information for now.

"My partner and I are part of a specialized police unit from London," Charley began. "Any extra information you can provide us with will only help to speed up your son's safe return."

"It's not like Herbert to go off on his own," said Mrs Fraser. "He's such a quiet boy normally, shy. Prefers it here with his father and me. Reads a lot of books..." A single teared rolled down the woman's round face.

"I won't keep you long. I know this must be very difficult for you," said Charley gently.

Mrs Fraser went to the window and pulled aside the curtain; looking out for her son and hiding her sadness.

"Did Constable Dunstable mention that two other boys have also disappeared in the last twenty-four hours?" asked Charley. "Arthur Smallbone and Fred Hawkins."

Mr Fraser nodded but said nothing.

"Did Herbert know the other boys?"

"Herbert kept himself to himself mostly," said Mrs Fraser. "I'm sure he'd seen Arthur Smallbone out and about, but they weren't friends or anything. And Fred Hawkins was a bit, you know..."

"Rough?" suggested Charley.

"The Hawkins family has fallen on hard times," said Mrs Fraser. "Fred's not a bad lad, but he's far more boisterous than our Herbert."

"So they didn't play together?" said Charley.

"Don't think so."

"And what about at school?" said Charley.

"Herbert's a real clever clogs," said Mrs Fraser, pride swelling her already ample bosom. "He goes to Milverton Hall. The Smallbone boy goes there too but he's in the year above our Herbert."

"And Fred Hawkins?"

"No," said Mrs Fraser. "Fred Hawkins is…" She struggled for the right word again and this time it was her husband who completed the sentence for her.

"A total buffoon, from what I've heard," said Mr Fraser, still wringing his hands as if they were wet and he couldn't get them dry. "Look, we've answered all these questions already. Constable Dunstable was here for nearly ten minutes. Are you any nearer to finding our boy?"

*Ten minutes*, thought Charley, *a thorough job*. "The more facts we can gather, the closer we get," she reassured him. Charley flicked to the next page of her notebook. "So how about you, Mr Fraser? Do you know the Smallbones or the Hawkinses? It might help if we could find some link between the missing boys."

*Let's just see if you mention the Chess Club*, thought Charley.

"I've seen them about," said Mr Fraser evasively. "Hobb's End is a small town."

"But you—" Mrs Fraser tried to add something but her husband cut her off.

"What my wife means to say is that I grew up in Hobb's End, so I'm bound to know *everybody*."

"I see," said Charley slowly. *So, it's like that, is it?* The thump of Billy's boots on the stairs told her that he had finished his part of the investigation. "We're nearly there now," she said. "Do you play chess, Mr Fraser?"

"I used to, back in my schooldays. Why?"

"Still does," said Mrs Fraser, "regular as clockwork."

Mr Fraser shot his wife a look. "Now and again," he said cagily.

That confirmed it for Charley – she didn't know how yet, but she was convinced that the Chess Club was connected to the disappearances.

"What is the point of these questions?" said Mr Fraser, trying to steer the conversation away from the subject of chess. "Shouldn't you be out searching for my son?"

"As you said, Constable Dunstable is already doing an excellent job of handling the manhunt." Charley paused and turned to Mrs Fraser. "When was the last time you saw Herbert?"

"When I tucked him up in bed," said Mrs Fraser, "with a mug of warm milk as always."

"So he didn't go to the carnival?"

"Oh no. Herbert was too quiet for that." A cloud of sadness passed over Mrs Fraser's face. "I remember pulling up his blanket and giving him a kiss. *Night, night, sleep tight, don't let the Hobb-Hound bite.*"

"The Hobb-Hound?"

"Just a silly story in these parts," said Mrs Fraser.

"You don't think it might have some basis in fact?"

"No," she said. "Although…"

"Although what, Mrs Fraser?"

"There was the one time when I was a little girl when I thought I saw something in the woods."

"Can you describe it for me?" asked Charley.

"It was a black dog, only it was enormous, bigger than any dog I've ever seen, before or since." She went quiet, her mind going back to that day. "It had red eyes, and they burned like fire—"

"Oh this is ridiculous!" snapped Mr Fraser. "A stupid local legend! You really are grasping at straws!"

"I'm sorry you think that," said Charley, "but I did mention that I am part of a specialized police unit."

"So you're telling me that the London police believe in goblins and ghoulies and things that go bump in the night?"

"Especially ghoulies!" said Billy, popping his head round the door.

"Thank you for your help, Mr Fraser," said Charley, bringing the interview to an end. "Goodbye." She wheeled away and then fired a parting shot over her shoulder. "Nice tie by the way!"

"Goodbye!" snapped Mr Fraser, crossing his arms firmly and leaving Mrs Fraser to show Charley and Billy to the front door.

"Old Ted is the one you should speak to if you want to find out about the Hobb-Hound," Mrs Fraser whispered as they were leaving. "Everyone in Hobb's End knows part of the legend but Old Ted's the expert. He lives down the lane, past the baker's. You'll know his house when you see it!"

"How can you be so sure?" asked Billy.

"Old Ted believes that light keeps the Hobb-Hound at bay and he's taking no chances!"

Outside and out of earshot, Charley and Billy compared notes.

"You look like the cat who got the cream, Billy. What did you find upstairs?"

"No claws marks on the window, I guess it must have been left open. But I did find this." He held up a test tube in which he had collected a small amount of liquid.

"What is that?" asked Charley, examining the clear fluid which stuck slimily to the sides of the glass.

"You're going to tell me when you've had a chance to examine it with your microscope, I hope," said Billy. "There were streaks of it all over the window sill. What did you come up with?"

"I think I've got a link between our missing boys."

Billy beamed. "Don't keep me in suspense."

"They don't know each other, but their *fathers* do."

"Go on."

"Did you see the major's cufflinks this morning?"

"Not really." Billy thought back. "Were they gold?"

"Yes, gold kings."

"Like Henry VIII?"

"No, like chess pieces."

"So?" Billy wasn't getting it.

"Would it surprise you to know that Mr Fraser was wearing a silver tiepin with a rook on it?"

"The castle-thingy?"

"Yes, Billy, the castle-thingy, and he was really defensive. He clearly didn't want to talk about it."

Billy slapped his forehead. "Mr Hawkins and the midnight Chess Club! So if the fathers know each other, then it means that their sons weren't kidnapped at random."

"No," said Charley. "Maybe this is personal... somehow."

"That's what we need to find out," said Billy. "Had Herbert been to the carnival?"

"No, Mrs Fraser was certain of that, although that doesn't mean that the carnival isn't connected. There's definitely something spooky about the zoetrope."

"That's where I'm off to now. I'm going to do some sneaking around behind the scenes and examine the zoetrope if I can get near it, hopefully question Dr Vindicta too. How about you?"

"First I'll pay a visit to this Old Ted character, see if

he can tell us more about the Hobb-Hound. Then I'm going to Milverton Hall, the school, to see what I can dig up there. Arthur Smallbone and Herbert Fraser both go there. Maybe their headmaster can shed some light on things? We said we'd meet Bunny at the tea rooms at three," said Charley, "so I'll see you there."

"Right you are."

"Hey," said Charley, catching her partner's arm as he turned to walk away. "Be careful."

"The worst the clowns can do is shove a pie in my face," he laughed. "And I like pies."

"And what's the worst a demon dog can do?"

Billy didn't answer that.

# CHAPTER ELEVEN

# THE LEGEND OF THE HOBB-HOUND

Just as Mrs Fraser had said, it was easy for Charley to find Old Ted's place. Her arms aching, she arrived outside a tumbledown cottage on the edge of the woods. Charley paused at the rickety garden gate. The tiny house was like something out of a fairy tale: lattice windows, smoke curling from the chimney, apple tree laden with fruit. The trouble for Charley was that she knew how all of those fairy tales ended: the apple was poisoned; the witch put the child in the oven; the wolf ate the granny right up.

What really struck Charley were the lamps which

burned in every window, even though it was morning and the autumn sky was clear blue. Cautiously Charley made her way up the path to the front door. Dozens of overripe apples lay on the ground and the air was buzzing with wasps drunk on cider. Charley got out her police badge and knocked. The net curtains at the window twitched and she spotted a man's face, as brown and withered as one of the rotting apples.

The door opened and a tiny woman stood there. No, Charley corrected herself, this woman was only tiny in height. She was probably fatter than she was tall, her pink sausage fingers wiping flour on her apron. Like the face she had seen at the window, the woman was brown and weather beaten, but her wrinkles all seemed to have been caused by smiling too much.

"I'm Detective Constable Charlotte Steel, S.C.R.E.A.M. squad," Charley introduced herself. "I'm looking for Old Ted. I'm told that he's an expert on local legends."

"I'm Lil," said the little old lady. "It's my brother you're after. Come on in, luvvie. Ted'll be pleased to see you." She waddled inside, her bottom swaying. "Ted loves to talk, it's getting him to shut up that's the problem."

After a brief struggle with the front step, Charley wheeled her way into the cottage. The ceilings were low and the exposed beams festooned with bunches of dried flowers. The air was thick with the welcoming smell of baking apple pie. There were more lamps inside, all lit in spite of the morning sunshine. Old Ted was seated at the kitchen table. He looked almost identical to his sister, except that his chin was slightly less hairy than hers and he only had two teeth in his mouth.

"Po-lice, eh?" said Old Ted, looking at Charley's badge. "This about those missing boys?"

"I see that I'm not going to be able to pull the wool over your eyes," said Charley.

"I know what they say in the town," said Old Ted, tapping the side of his head. "I know they say that Old Ted has bats in the belfry. But I ain't mad."

"No," said Lil. "Spendin' yer whole life searching for a demon dog ain't mad at all."

"Well, I'm glad you mentioned the Hobb-Hound," said Charley. "I'm told you're the expert on the subject."

"Expert?" said Old Ted with false modesty. "I wouldn't say that."

"Neither would I," said Lil with a grin. "Detective, would you like a dish of tea? I've got the kettle on."

"That would be wonderful," said Charley. "Earl Grey if you've got it."

Lil's face fell.

"Actually, I've changed my mind, sorry. What tea have you got?" Charley asked.

"Normal tea or rosehip," said Lil, her smile returning.

"Rosehip tea would be delightful," said Charley.

Lil went off to make it and the jolly old man pulled his chair nearer to the kitchen table. He leaned forward. "What do you want to know about the demon dog of Hobb's End?"

Charley opened her notebook and pulled out a freshly sharpened pencil. "I'd like the whole story, please."

Old Ted cleared his throat. "No one knows which came first, the town or the hound, but Hobb's End has always lived in its shadow."

Lil returned with the tea and some cups and saucers on a tray. "I've used my best china, since we've got a guest."

Old Ted poured three cups and pushed one towards Charley. "There's this old rhyme, you see, and it goes like this:

"'*Beware the monster of the night, that feeds on vengeance, hate and fright.*

"'*It searches far, it searches near, it sniffs you out and smells your fear.*

106

"'*So when the sun comes out to play, all the boys have gone away,*

"'*Taken swiftly in the night, when the Hobb-Hound takes to flight!*'"

Old Ted frowned. "You didn't write that down."

"Sorry," said Charley, "but I've already heard it."

Old Ted looked crestfallen.

"You know more than that though, don't you?" she said hopefully, wondering if she was wasting her time. While the old man recomposed himself, Charley took her cup politely and sipped the sweet, fragrant tea. On the opposite side of the table, Old Ted tipped the tea out of his cup and splashed it into his saucer, then he brought it to his lips and sucked the hot liquid into his toothless mouth. For a second, Charley was mesmerized by the disgusting sight and sounds of the old man's flapping lips.

"The Hobb-Hound's real, I know that much," he said at last.

Charley was relieved that Ted's saucer was empty and he didn't refill it. "How can you be so sure?" she asked.

He chuckled. "Didn't you hear it last night? Wasn't that howl proof enough?"

"I heard the howling, but that isn't evidence of the Hobb-Hound. Your sister said that you've been searching all your life, what have you uncovered in that time?"

"Boys have gone missing before," he said slowly, "just like in the rhyme, taken in the night they were."

"Who?" said Charley, sitting bolt upright. "When?"

"Their names were John Scott Hope, Anthony Parsons, Henry Wood, and Neville Forester. Never seen again, any of 'em." Old Ted's face grew dark. He blew into his hands. "Disappeared into thin air."

Charley was pushing down on her pencil so hard that the lead snapped. "When was this? Why didn't Constable Dunstable mention it?"

"Before the constable's time," said Old Ted.

"He's only been here ten years," chipped in Lil.

"So the disappearances happened when exactly?" asked Charley.

"Nearly fifty years ago," said Old Ted. "Then there was the Doyle boys, they went missing too. That was even further back, mind you."

"And none of these boys was ever seen again?" said Charley.

Ted shook his head.

In her notebook Charley crossed out the word *kidnapped* and replaced it with *stolen*. Stolen, presumed dead. "But no disappearances in the last fifty years?"

"No," said Old Ted. "Not one. The Hobb-Hound is patient, all the demon dogs are."

"*All* the demon dogs?"

"Aye," said Old Ted. "There's demon dogs from Land's End to John o' Groats. There's the 'Gurt Dog' of Somerset, for a start; 'Moddey Dhoo' is the phantom hound of the Isle of Man; and the dreaded 'Cù Sìth' stalks the Highlands of Scotland.

"Fascinating." Charley didn't have the heart to tell him that she had already read about all these demons and more in the books which Luther Sparkwell had supplied for this case.

"'The Grim' is a truly terrifying dog demon," said Old Ted. "It follows lost travellers down lonely lanes. An' there's the 'Padfoot' which stalks graveyards, pouncing on the heartbroken, and 'Black Shuck', the one-eyed cyclops hound. Monsters, all of them. Drawn to fear and misery like flies to cowpats."

"Not man's best friend then?"

"Not these damned dogs," he said. "Way back in 1577 the Black Dog of Bungay terrorized St Mary's church, breaking down the door in the middle of a thunderstorm and snapping the necks of the poor folks inside! The descriptions of the demon dogs are always the same. Big, black and nasty. I can vouch for that." Old Ted's voice lowered to little more than a croak. "I've seen the Hobb-Hound."

"So have I," said Lil.

"Yes," said Old Ted, "but I saw it first."

"We was only small at the time," said Lil. "We'd been out playing in the fields and we'd lost track of time. Night was falling so we took a shortcut through the woods. That was a mistake." She trembled at the memory. "We got lost. We'd never been so afraid. It was then that we heard movement in the darkness behind us."

"Like I said," cut in Old Ted. "Drawn to fear."

"Anyway," Lil continued, "we turned around and there it was – an enormous black hound stalking us."

"As big as the biggest wolfhound you've ever seen," said Old Ted. "Seven foot from nose to tail."

"Bigger," said Lil enthusiastically. "Ten foot. As big as a horse. A really, really big horse."

"Yes, maybe," said Old Ted less enthusiastically. "Anyhow it was big and it had these horrible red eyes."

"Glowing they were, like the lamps of Hell itself!"

"Tongue lolling from its mouth," Old Ted added, grabbing his story back. "Great strings of slobber spilling from its chops. And on its back, you'll never guess—"

"WINGS!" Lil blurted out, earning a vicious glare from her brother for stealing his thunder. "Wings like a bat!"

"Anyway, we ran and ran as if our lives depended on it."

"How on earth did you escape?" asked Charley.

"Sheer luck," admitted the old man. "We managed to find our way home, our legs scratched to pieces from all the brambles we'd blundered through, but by this time the Hobb-Hound nearly had us. Wings flapping. Jaws snapping! Breathing down our necks! We wanted to get into the house but the outdoor toilet was closer and so we both bundled in there."

"Mam always lit a lantern in the lav in the night-time and that was what saved us," said Lil.

"The Hobb-Hound tore down the door and we thought we were goners," said Old Ted. "I don't know what I was thinking, but I grabbed the lantern and sort of shoved it in the demon's face. Well it didn't like that,

I can tell you. It backed off, hissing and growling. So I waved the lantern again—"

"And you dropped it!" Lil cut in. "The oil went everywhere and the toilet shed caught on fire. It flared right up and that was what scared the Hobb-Hound off! It leaped into the air and flew away!"

"Did your mam see it too?" asked Charley.

"No," said Old Ted. "And I got a terrible telling-off for burning down our toilet."

"When was this?" said Charley.

"A lifetime ago," said Old Ted. "I was only a nipper of four."

"And I was five," finished Lil. "I remember it like it was yesterday. We've kept the lamps burning ever since."

"Light is what hurts it," said Old Ted. "You remember that." He handed Charley an ancient scrap of parchment. "You should have this."

Charley took it gently. "What is it?"

"Some words that will protect you, I hope. Found them in an ancient book."

From the beautiful handwriting and the frailty of the paper, Charley guessed that it was a medieval enchantment.

Do not let your hearts be troubled.
Do not be afraid.
When the dark dog draws near,
A courageous soul shall cast out fear.

"Thank you," said Charley. "You've been very helpful."

"And they do say," continued Lil, her excitement bubbling away like jam on the stove, "that if you leave a tooth under your pillow, the Hobb-Hound will take it in the night and leave a shiny sixpence in its place!"

Old Ted glared. "That's the tooth fairy, you silly old boot! Honestly," he said, rolling his eyes. "And they say *I'm* the barmy one!"

Old Ted escorted Charley to the door, then hesitated, his gentle expression growing suddenly serious. "You find those boys, missy," he said. "Find 'em before they're lost for ever."

# CHAPTER TWELVE

# A DEAL WITH A DEMON

Charley's words echoed in Billy's ears all the way to Dr Vindicta's Carnival of Monsters. *Last day!* it said on the signs. *Leaving tomorrow.* That wasn't good. The clock was ticking.

The carnival seemed different in daylight. The bunting was tattered and faded. The clowns in their make-up appeared tired rather than scary. However, the children and townsfolk of Hobb's End were keen to make the most of it. Just as excited, just as scared, just as quick to be parted with their money. All unaware that they could be in terrible danger from whatever evil was lurking in the zoetrope.

Billy wanted to blow his police whistle, to tell them to go home, that the fun was over. But he knew that would only end in panic. Worse than that, the carnival folk would pack up and be on their way before he and Charley solved the mystery and rescued those boys.

Billy blended in with the crowd, but he needed a way to go behind the scenes and investigate. As soon as no one was looking, he slipped behind the tents and made his way over to the brightly painted caravans, where the carnival folk lived. First, he needed a disguise.

Crouching low, Billy tucked himself down against one of the caravan wheels, careful not to startle the nearby horses and give himself away. He listened for any sign of movement inside. If he walked in on someone he could always use his police badge to explain his presence, but the news that the police were there would spread through the carnival like wildfire; his cover would be blown.

As sure as he could be that the caravan was empty, Billy climbed the short ladder and opened the door. Then he froze, half in and half out.

The caravan was occupied after all. *Blast!*

The curtains were drawn at the small windows and Billy could make out a figure sitting directly opposite him beside the stove. It was too late to run away, so Billy took another step closer. "I'm a police officer."

The figure remained motionless.

"Don't be alarmed," Billy repeated.

The only answer was a snore.

Quickly, Billy snatched the clown's outfit off the back of the door and got out while the going was good.

Still cautious not to be spotted, Billy rolled underneath the caravan. He knew it was a mistake as soon as he had done it. He had rolled in a heap of manure. The horses whinnied.

"Very funny," he said. "Perhaps one day I'll poo in the street and let *you* walk in it."

Billy slipped out of his own filthy trousers and struggled into the costume. It was a tatty old thing, with a black cloak and a hood with eyeholes which came down over Billy's face like a half-mask. The costume reeked of sweat, just like the caravan, but beggars couldn't be choosers.

Crawling on hands and knees, Billy emerged from his hiding place. The coast was clear and he was swiftly up on his feet, moving quickly but keeping it casual. *I belong here, I'm one of the team*; that's what he hoped his walk said.

Billy headed straight for Dr Vindicta's tent and the zoetrope. His face was sweating underneath the woollen cowl of the costume, but he started to shiver as he got closer, his skin rising in goosebumps. The tent was fastened shut, the flaps down and a sign said that the Wheel of the Devil was closed for maintenance. Billy didn't believe that for one moment. It was closed because something was happening inside. Now that he was nearer, Billy could hear a heated conversation coming from behind the canvas wall. He loitered by the door, bending down and pretending to tie his boot laces while his ears strained to hear what was going on.

There were two voices. The first was full of fear. "Can we call it off?" the man pleaded. "You said you were my friend."

"You signed the contract," snarled the second voice, as deep and dangerous as a mineshaft. "I have nearly completed my side of the bargain."

"But I don't want this any more. I thought I did but I've changed my mind."

"You signed the contract," the growling voice repeated. "Arthur Smallbone, Fred Hawkins, Herbert Fraser, Sidney Coldblood, those were the names that you gave me—"

"Yes, but—"

"I have taken three of those children already. One more, the last, and then I shall have MY payment."

Outside, Billy was trembling as his sixth sense was alerted. The sensation was almost overwhelming. He was in the presence of true wickedness. Biting his lip, Billy lay on his belly and tried to lift the canvas. He *had* to see inside...

"I want out!" the first voice squealed. "I can't go through with it!"

"You signed the contract," the second voice growled.

"But I built all of this for *you*! Isn't that enough?"

Billy had lifted the side of the tent just enough to look with one eye, and hopefully not be spotted. What he saw filled him with dread, like a cold hand squeezing his heart.

The zoetrope wasn't broken. It was spinning wildly, an impossible blur of movement. The metal skeleton was winding the handle furiously, thin columns of smoke rising from the ball bearings of its metal joints. And as the zoetrope spun Billy could see three boys – *could it really be them?* – in silhouette, all running in a never-ending circle.

The centre of the wheel had become a swirling circle

of magical energy. Blue flames writhed. Sparks of spectral energy arced and flashed, like electricity. As the zoetrope spun faster, so the silhouette-boys' panic grew. Billy couldn't see their expressions, but the boys' actions spoke loudly enough. They were desperate to escape. The zoetrope stopped spinning and the boys were now frantically hammering on the paper wheel with their fists.

As a police officer, Billy had seen grown men act in exactly the same way – pounding their fists on a prison door after it had slammed shut and they realized their fate.

That must be it, Billy realized. The zoetrope was some sort of magic prison. The lost boys were trapped inside!

Standing beside the zoetrope, Billy saw a short, scruffy man, with thinning hair and a weak chin. Whoever he was, Billy didn't recognize him.

He didn't look for long, though, because he couldn't take his eyes off the huge black dog that was walking in slow circles around the little man. It was like no dog that Billy had ever seen. The torso and front legs looked more human than canine, lean and muscular beneath a coat of black fur. The front paws were like elongated hands ending in deadly talons – *sharp enough to leave those scratch marks on Arthur's window sill.* The back legs were totally dog-like though, and so was the tail swishing from side to side between them. On its back were a pair of leathery wings. The head was that of a monstrous hound, with swept back ears, and a mouth full of yellowing teeth. Billy caught a flash of the creature's eyes. They were fiercely intelligent and they blazed with red fire.

But the burning eyes were not the worst thing about it.

Billy's stomach twisted with fright as he listened – the dog was talking.

*The Hobb-Hound, it has to be!* thought Billy.

He put the pieces together. The zoetrope was more than a prison, it was a gateway too! A door between this realm and a dimension of demons! A door which the Hobb-Hound could come through, but which kept the kidnapped boys trapped on the other side.

Strings of drool poured from between the Hobb-Hound's teeth. The jaws moved, the lips curled and a deep voice boomed out. "I shall have my payment; *I shall have your soul!*"

At that moment Billy jumped out of his skin. Not because of the Hobb-Hound's monstrous threat, but because a heavy hand had landed on his shoulder! Billy didn't have time to react before he was jerked to his feet. He was too stunned to speak. He had been so wrapped up in what he was seeing that he had failed to realize that someone was sneaking up on him! He spun round and was face-to-face with one of Dr Vindicta's clowns.

"There you are, Khulan," said the clown, steering Billy away with a strong arm around his shoulders. "We can't keep the crowd waiting. You're on!"

"On what?" Billy mumbled.

"Blimey, maybe you did hit your head in that last show!" the big clown laughed. "You're the one and only Khulan Cannonball! It's time for you to do some flying!"

# CHAPTER THIRTEEN

## THE BEST DAYS OF YOUR LIFE

Milverton Hall was a bleak, grey building. It reminded Charley of a prison, with its heavy iron gates and tall surrounding walls. But the boys in the playground were laughing and joking as they played with marbles and spinning tops, jumping jacks and swords made out of sticks. A boy with a grazed knee and a cheeky smile showed Charley to the headmaster's office. "Mr Walnut is in 'ere, Miss," he said and then he ran off, probably to scrape the skin off his *other* knee, Charley thought with a smile.

She knocked and when the reply came she wheeled in.

The small man behind the desk suited his name; he was shrivelled and dry. His face was a mask of wrinkles and his two tiny black eyes peered at Charley from behind half-moon glasses.

"I'm Detective Constable Charlotte Steel," she said, showing the headmaster her S.C.R.E.A.M. badge. "I think you can help me with my enquiries, Mr Walnut."

"It's Mr *Warner*," he corrected with a scowl. Then the crinkly face softened. "The children will have their little joke." He squinted at her ID badge. "Supernatural crimes, rescues, emergencies *and* mysteries. My, my, I imagine that keeps you very busy," Mr Warner chuckled sarcastically. "How can I help you, detective?"

"Three boys have gone missing, Mr Warner."

"Three?" said Mr Warner, screwing his eyes up tight in thought. "I was aware of Arthur Smallbone and Herbert Fraser. Who is the third?"

"Fred Hawkins."

"Ahhh, not a Milverton Hall boy," he said, as if that made it better.

Charley found herself disliking this shrivelled prune of a man more and more. "Fred goes to the church school."

"With all the other raggedy boys and girls," said Mr Warner with a hint of self-satisfaction.

"Tell me about Arthur and Herbert," said Charley, biting back her annoyance. "Are they friends?"

"Not especially."

"Do they share any interests? Go to the same clubs?"

"No."

"Do they stand out at all?" asked Charley, searching for a reason why the Hobb-Hound might have taken them, beyond the link between their fathers. "Is there anything different about these boys?"

"Nothing comes to mind."

Charley gritted her teeth. This line of questioning was getting her nowhere.

"How long you have been here, Mr Warner?"

"All my life."

"So I suppose you've known some of the adults in Hobb's End since they were children," said Charley, with the feeling that she might be on to something.

"Yes indeed. It makes me feel ancient when the grown man who serves me in the greengrocer's turns out to be a boy that I was beating with my cane only yesterday." Mr Warner sighed as if it was a fond memory.

"Do you remember all of your former pupils?"

"Oh no, there are far too many of them. I recall only the brightest and the best – or the very worst."

"Did you teach Herbert Fraser's father by any chance? He was a Milverton Hall boy."

The old headmaster's face wrinkled in thought until his eyes almost disappeared completely. "I did."

"What about Arthur Smallbone's father and Fred Hawkins's?"

"They were Milverton boys too, I'm sorry to say." Mr Warner got up from his desk and walked over to the window, looking out over the playing fields, his back to Charley, his face hidden.

"Were they friends?"

"Yes."

"Did they play chess together?" asked Charley eagerly.

Warner paused and then answered: "No, they did not. Chess is a game for *gentlemen*, Detective Steel. Smallbone, Hawkins and Fraser never played chess. Those..." Charley thought the old headmaster was about to swear. "Those *foolish* boys called themselves the 'Chess Club' but all they ever played was the clown..."

"What do you mean?"

"Jokes. Japes. Tomfoolery!" Warner spat the words as if they tasted bad in his mouth.

"What sort of jokes?" asked Charley.

"What possible relevance can it have?"

"Please, Mr Warner, whatever you tell me might help me to rescue the missing boys."

The old headmaster returned from the window wearily, the black cloak of his gown flapping around him. "The Chess Club thought it was funny to play pranks. Can you imagine that, Detective Steel? Pranks *in school*?" Warner made a noise to suggest that the very idea of having fun would be the end of the world as he knew it. "High jinks! Monkeyshines! All that malarkey!"

"What do you mean?"

"Foolishness, Detective Steel. Putting jam on a boy's head at the school picnic so the wasps chased him. Itching powder inside shorts. Buckets of water balanced on doors. Tricking people into eating dried slugs and telling them that it was liquorice!"

"So if I'm getting this right, the Chess Club played practical jokes on other children?"

"They positively delighted in it!" said Warner. "Smallbone was the ringleader, he called himself the king—"

*The king!* Charley thought of the major's cufflinks.

"Hawkins was the knight and Fraser was the rook. And there was one more member of their silly little gang…"

"Who?" Charley urged. "Please try to remember."

"Coldblood, that's it!" said Mr Warner, slapping his forehead. "He was the bishop."

Charley's mind was racing – that confirmed it; the lost boys weren't connected, but their fathers were – all part of the so-called "Chess Club". Could one of their victims be behind the kidnappings? she wondered. "Was there anyone in particular who they liked to tease?"

"Too many to count. They called them their 'pawns', just like the weakest pieces on a chessboard. I suppose they thought that was funny too?" said Mr Warner. "But I do recall one poor lad who had more than his fair share of their practical jokes." Mr Warner rubbed his chin as the memories came back to him. "Small boy, bit of a cry baby, as I recall. His name was Parker…Patrick Parker."

"Thank you," said Charley. As much as she disliked the casual cruelty of teachers like Mr Warner, that piece of information might prove to be a vital clue. "What else do you remember of Parker?"

"Bit sad really. Two dead parents and an inheritance which paid for his education at Milverton Hall but didn't leave a single penny to spare." Mr Warner pinched his lips together. "Patrick Parker was an unremarkable student and a hopeless athlete. Couldn't kick a ball or run without getting wheezy! But he did have a passion and a gift for horology."

"The art and science of measuring time," said Charley.

"Indeed," said Mr Warner approvingly. "I see you have some knowledge of the classics."

"Patrick Parker?" Charley prompted.

"Yes, Parker had this gold watch, the only reminder of his late mother and father or some such. Anyway, the boy spent every hour taking the watch apart and then putting it back together again. He even got himself an interview with a prestigious horologist. If he'd become an apprentice watchmaker, Parker would have been set up for life."

"I take it he didn't pass the interview."

"No," said Mr Warner.

"Why? If he knew so much about watches?"

"You may have noticed a rather handsome house next to the school, Detective Steel?"

"I could hardly miss it," said Charley. "The one with the walled garden?"

"That's *my* house," said Mr Warner, "and on the day of his interview the Chess Club thought it would be funny if they pulled off Parker's trousers and then threw them over my garden wall."

"I don't suppose Parker laughed much."

"No, I don't suppose he did," said Mr Warner. "Back then I had an Irish wolfhound named Captain and from what I found out from the boys afterwards, Parker scrambled over my wall after his trousers and then spent an hour with Captain chasing him round the garden in his underpants. Mostly yelping. And squealing. With a little bit of crying too."

"But I still don't understand. Why did Parker lose his apprenticeship? Surely he could have explained what happened to the watchmaker?"

"He tried to. I even wrote a letter on his behalf. But the one thing the watchmaker could never forgive was lateness."

"So," said Charley. "A stupid prank by the Chess Club ruined Parker's chances."

"Parker the Pawn," said Mr Warner. "I wonder what became of him?"

# CHAPTER FOURTEEN

# MAN-BAT!

"Roll up, roll up! Prepare to be amazed by our human cannonball, Khulan the Incredible!" The crowd roared with anticipation and delight.

Billy was not delighted. Not one little bit. Billy was scared.

The clown who had found him loitering outside Dr Vindicta's tent was a big man with hands the size of shovels and a firm grip on Billy's shoulders. Billy had mumbled a few excuses, but he couldn't risk speaking much for fear of being uncovered as an intruder. As always, he could simply reveal himself to be a police officer and demand to be let go. However if the whole carnival was involved in the kidnappings then all he would achieve would be to land himself in more trouble.

No, Billy decided, he just had to brave it out. After all, how difficult could it be to be fired out of a cannon?

The clown with the big hands, whose face was made up to resemble a rotting corpse, shoved Billy forward into the ring. "Take a bow," the clown hissed. "I'll get the ladder and then it's up you go!"

Billy staggered forward into the circus ring. There were dozens of people gawping and pointing. Billy felt exposed. It was unpleasant to be the focus of so many eyes and he felt a stab of sympathy for the bearded lady and all the other carnival folk who made their livings being pointed and jeered at. With no other choice than to play along, Billy flung out his arms to reveal the bat wings of his costume and took a bow. The crowd cheered even louder.

Peering out through the eye-slits in his black hood, Billy turned to look at the cannon. The barrel was massive; Billy wasn't sure whether that was good or bad. Two more clowns, one with a werewolf mask and the other dressed as a zombie, were at the business end making the final preparations to launch him into the sky.

Billy scanned the ring and spotted the net at the far end which was meant to catch him. The distance was probably only a hundred feet, but it seemed miles away.

Billy felt that familiar heavy hand nudging him in the back and he walked over to the ladder which had been propped up against the barrel. The long barrel was aiming up into the sky at a forty-five degree angle, like an accusing finger. He climbed up slowly, one rung at a time, although he knew he was only delaying the inevitable. At the top he hesitated, and then put his head into the open mouth of the barrel.

"Feet first, you numbskull!" shouted the clown from the bottom of the ladder. "And don't forget to keep your legs straight. You don't want to break them like the *last* human cannonball!"

Billy did some manoeuvring and somehow managed to get himself from the top of the ladder and into the mouth of the cannon without falling. The barrel was tighter than Billy had imagined. He instantly felt trapped and had to fight down his growing sense of panic as gravity pulled him down deeper into the cold metal tunnel until his feet were resting on the bottom. There was no room to move. Billy's arms were pointing straight upwards and instinctively he folded them around his head – it wouldn't be much protection if he missed the net, but it was all that he could do.

Billy had no idea how the cannon actually worked, but he could smell gunpowder, and he knew that he was about to find out the hard way. It was dark inside the barrel, like being at the bottom of a well with only a circle of light above him. Although it was muffled, Billy could hear the happy laughter of the crowd. There was a drum roll and the countdown began.

*FIVE!*

Billy calmed his mind…

*FOUR!*

Billy tensed his body, ready for the impact which he knew was coming…

*THREE!*

Billy said a quiet prayer…

*TWO!*

Billy locked his legs out straight…

*ONE!*

Billy squeezed his buttocks together…

*FIRE!*

Billy screamed. He couldn't help it.

A rush of compressed air punched him out of the barrel and into the sky. It was painful. A solid whack against his feet and legs, like the worst belly flop he'd ever done. Times ten. But Billy didn't have much time to think about his dead legs – he was too busy falling.

At the back of his mind Billy was aware that he should keep his body straight, like a diver, but would it help if he put his arms out, spreading the bat wings of his costume? Everything was happening too fast though, so instead he opted for a mixture of random flapping and plummeting…hopefully not to his death!

Whatever, he thought. It would all be over soon.

Beneath him the crowd were holding their breath. Perhaps it was their first time seeing a young police officer dressed as a flying mouse travelling through the air at sixty miles an hour?

Now the net was rushing up towards Billy. It was full of holes.

The tiny part of his mind that was thinking rationally sent an urgent warning to his arms and legs and at the last instant Billy tucked himself up into a ball. If one of his limbs went through the net at the wrong angle it would snap like a twig.

Billy hit the net – YES!

Then bounced back up into the air again – NO!

His stomach was doing somersaults. It wouldn't be

much of a grand finale if he vomited all over himself, although it might tone down the stench of manure which still made him gag, even as he flew.

Billy bounced three more times, but each rebound was smaller than the last and finally the net came to rest and Billy was down.

He half-climbed, half-fell off the net and as soon as his feet were safely on the ground the crowd went wild. Billy took their applause. Bowed twice. And then made a run for it.

He'd had enough of these clowns.

# CHAPTER FIFTEEN

# LET SLEEPING DOGS LIE

**B**illy made his excuses as the crowd called out for more and stumbled back in the direction of the caravans. His stomach was churning after his death-defying flight and he was quite glad to be out of earshot as his bottom let out a thunderous fart of sheer relief.

He had to put the horrifying experience behind him now though, and focus on the case. He wanted to get a closer look at the zoetrope. First he stripped off his disguise and reclaimed his own clothes. They stank of manure but Billy was past caring; as long as he wasn't mistaken for "Khulan the Incredible" ever again.

The *Closed for maintenance* sign was still outside the zoetrope tent. Making sure that no one could see him, Billy kneeled beside the canvas and listened carefully. Nothing. The man had gone and so had the Hobb-Hound, thank God. Coast clear, Billy lifted the edge of the tent and wormed his way inside, crawling on his belly.

The huge zoetrope dominated the tent. The Grim Reaper was motionless. There were no silhouettes. There was no movement. Still, Billy felt uncomfortable as he approached it, as if he was creeping up on a sleeping guard dog and daren't risk waking it.

Cautiously Billy stepped closer. He and Charley had investigated old mansion houses where the stones still held the memory of terrible things that had happened within their walls. The zoetrope was like that. Although it was only paper and wood on a metal frame, this spinning wheel was an evil thing. A prison. And the missing boys were trapped inside, Billy was convinced of it.

The zoetrope seemed even more sinister now that Billy knew its secret. Part of him wanted to set fire to it, to destroy the wicked thing. But how could he with Arthur and Fred and Herbert still inside?

Billy glanced nervously over his shoulder. He had already been caught off guard once and had no idea how much time he had to investigate. The Grim Reaper was standing silently and Billy moved swiftly to give it a quick once-over. "'Scuse me, darlin'," he said, lifting up the hem of the monk-like robes to see what secrets he could find underneath.

Inside the dummy's metal ribcage was a complex array of cogs, wheels and springs. Billy let the robe drop. That was one question answered, anyway. The Grim Reaper was nothing more than a mechanical mannequin.

While his luck was still holding – if you didn't count getting fired from a giant cannon – Billy walked all the way around the edge of the zoetrope. He examined its paper walls. He touched the slits. He ran his hands over its cold surface, feeling the tremble in the tips of his fingers. But all the time he was careful not to set the wheel spinning by accident – God only knew what might happen then.

Satisfied that he could extract nothing more from outside the zoetrope, Billy got down on his hands and knees and crawled inside. The mechanics of the zoetrope were exactly what he expected. There was a solid central spindle, and emerging from that hub, like spokes from a wheel, were thinner metal rods which supported the lightweight paper and wood of the wheel itself. What Billy hadn't been expecting was the writing, scrawled in a single sentence around the interior. The words were hidden from the outside, but now that Billy was inside the zoetrope they were impossible to miss.

The letters stood a foot high. They weren't written in the alphabet that Billy had learned in school, but it was clear that they were not random scribbles either. They had been added with intensity, ferocity even. The strokes were bold and strong. Was this the contract that the Hobb-Hound had spoken of?

The ink – *please let it be ink* – was deep, dark red. Billy couldn't read a word of it but every instinct told him that what it said was very nasty indeed.

His studies under Luther Sparkwell had given Billy knowledge which few other people ever had. He knew that in monasteries in the snow-capped mountains of Tibet the monks carved prayers onto wheels which they spun, sending their words of blessing and peace into the world.

Maybe Dr Vindicta's zoetrope was some kind of prayer wheel too. But when it spun, the incantation it released was full of hate.

# CHAPTER SIXTEEN

# BUBBLE, BUBBLE, WE'RE IN TROUBLE

Charley returned to the Smallbone house, her mind running over what she had learned. This was turning out to be a deeper mystery than she had first imagined. Some cases were simple – not *easy*, tackling supernatural entities was never easy – but certainly straightforward. Find the creature, stop the creature doing the unpleasant thing it was doing; go home; case closed. But the case of the Carnival of Monsters was getting deeper and darker by the moment.

Lost in thought, Charley let herself into the house. Pausing only to make herself a cup of steaming hot tea, she returned to her room and looked at the sample which Billy had collected from Herbert Fraser's window sill. The slimy liquid sloshed back and forth in the test tube as if it had a life of its own.

Charley and Billy both travelled well prepared when they were on a mission. Billy's special equipment was mainly supplied by Luther Sparkwell. In his satchel Charley knew that Billy was carrying all sorts of defences against the supernatural. Plus a catapult and a penknife, because Billy was the sort of boy who *always* had a catapult and a penknife. Charley's equipment came straight from the British Scientific Institute. She had the finest microscope that money could buy. It had been crucial in solving a number of mysteries. She fondly remembered proving that it was a yeti *not* a werewolf which had been responsible for terrorizing a small Scottish island, just by identifying a single hair found at the scene of the crime.

Today however she would need her chemistry set. Humming to herself, Charley spent a happy twenty minutes assembling a complex arrangement of retort stands and flasks, joined together by the beautiful spiral of a condensing tube. In her own laboratory, Charley had a Bunsen burner for when she needed to heat chemicals, but when she was travelling she had to make do with an oil burner. She positioned it beneath the test tube holding the strange slime.

Charley heated the sample gently and then watched in fascination as it bubbled and boiled, turning from a liquid into a gas. The gas travelled through the network of tubes, turning back into a liquid again and dripping from the condenser into a waiting Petri dish. Charley dipped a strip of litmus paper into the liquid and smiled to herself as it changed from blue to red. The liquid was an acid.

She held the litmus paper carefully between thumb and forefinger to ensure she didn't contaminate the sample. What happened next made her drop the paper in shock.

Where the test paper had turned red it was now disappearing entirely!

It was quite fascinating, once she had recovered from her initial surprise. Acid didn't make things disappear within seconds. If the acid was strong enough it might burn or melt an object. But even hydrochloric or sulphuric acid couldn't destroy something so quickly.

Charley rubbed her chin thoughtfully.

She had some more experiments to perform.

# CHAPTER SEVENTEEN

# SCREAM TEA

Charley checked her pocket watch. Billy and Bunny were late. They had arranged to meet at the tea room on the High Street at three o'clock sharp. Fortunately she had her notebook with her, so the time wasn't completely wasted.

It was now thirty-five minutes past four. Thirty-*six*.

The bell above the door tinkled and Billy almost fell in. He looked in a terrible state.

"What time do you call this?" She tapped her watch and smiled. Then her small nose wrinkled as she smelled the waft of manure, gunpowder and sweat which Billy brought with him to the table. "And what *have* you been doing?"

"It's a long story," he said, as he flopped down in the chair opposite her, exhausted.

Charley was on her second pot of tea and she saw her partner's eyes widen when he spotted the cake trolley. Charley waved the waitress over. "Scones, jam and cream for two please."

"With extra jam. And extra cream," said Billy. "And an extra scone."

Charley raised an eyebrow.

"What?" said Billy. "Fighting evil gives me an appetite."

"Any excuse," said Charley. She opened her notebook with satisfaction. "I've made some useful discoveries."

"So have I," said Billy, through a mouthful of scone.

"I'll go first," said Charley. "It's either that or get showered with crumbs."

Billy took another enormous mouthful, cream oozing from the corners of his mouth.

"I met an old man with no teeth, horrible drinking habits, but a headful of knowledge about the Hobb-Hound," said Charley. "I got two excellent pieces of information from him. Firstly, that the Hobb-Hound feeds on fear—"

"Like a sort of psychic vampire, only instead of drinking blood it sucks up emotions – ughhh." Billy grimaced at the thought.

"And secondly, the Hobb-Hound is afraid of light. Ted's own experience hinted that light *might* even work as a weapon against it."

"Useful," said Billy.

"That's what I thought," said Charley. "Also, I've had the chance to analyse that slime you found on the window sill at Mr and Mrs Fraser's."

"What was it?"

"Mostly water, but with traces of electrolytes, mucus, anti-bacterial compounds, various aggressive enzymes and an ectoplasmic element."

"And in English that means?"

"Saliva. Or more specifically demon drool."

"Yuck. That's almost enough to put me off my lunch." Still, Billy continued spooning a small mountain of clotted cream onto a scone and topping it off with strawberry jam. "*Almost.*"

"It has some unique properties," Charley continued. "Not least of which is that it can make matter disappear entirely."

"When you say 'matter' what do you mean?" said

Billy through a mouthful of scone.

"Organic matter. Plant or animal life or products."

"You mean *people*, don't you? You think that the Hobb-Hound has eaten the missing boys."

Charley nodded. "As horrible as it is, we have to be prepared for the possibility that Arthur, Fred and Herbert have been…dissolved."

"Don't give up hope, Duchess. Whatever has happened to the lost boys there is still a chance that we can get them back alive."

"But if they've been digested?"

"Something terrible *has* happened to them, that's the truth," said Billy. "But from what I've seen at the carnival, I'm positive that they didn't end up as a dog's dinner."

"How can you know that?"

"I'm pretty sure that I know what the zoetrope is."

"Really! Do tell."

"It's a dimensional gate, between our world and the spirit world. The boys have been taken through and they're trapped inside, while the Hobb-Hound can move in and out."

Charley's brow furrowed in thought. "So it's a prison for the boys, but a magic revolving door for the Hobb-Hound? But how would that work?"

"How does any magic work?" said Billy. "We just know that it does. My theory is that the weedy-looking bloke I saw *made* the zoetrope, but it has to be the Hobb-Hound's power behind it. And if it is working as a *prison* as well as a gateway, then surely only the Devil himself could make that happen." Billy paused. It was a lot to take in. "I wonder? Something you said about the demon slime—"

"Ectoplasmic element."

"That *stuff* makes things disappear, yes?"

"Yes."

"But what if, instead of dissolving things completely, it *changes* them?"

Charley grabbed his train of thought and ran with it. "It's not scientifically impossible," she said. "There are countless chemical reactions which change the state of matter, from solid to liquid for example, or liquid to gas. So what you're saying is that the saliva from the Hobb-Hound didn't *destroy* our missing boys, but *changed* them from solid into…what exactly?"

"I don't know," said Billy. "But they're trapped inside the paper prison of the zoetrope. That's why my sixth sense reacted to the wheel last night. It wasn't the Hobb-Hound setting it off, it was the magical nature of the zoetrope itself."

"It also explains why the silhouette performed a different routine each time. And why Newt was so convinced she saw Fred Hawkins! The silhouettes are living shadows." Charley smiled. "Good detective work, partner."

"I've got loads more where that came from," said Billy, spraying scone.

"I speak, you listen," said Charley playfully. She made a show of getting a crisp white handkerchief and wiping down her notebook. She bent the book open, making the leather spine squeak. "Now where was I? Ah yes, I think I've found the link between the missing boys. Their fathers went to school together and from what the headmaster told me they were pretty mean when they were young."

Billy pushed the last morsel of scone into his mouth and then wiped his lips on a napkin for Charley's benefit. "The Chess Club?"

"Yes, but they didn't play chess, they played jokes. There was one particular trick which went too far—"

The tea room door opened then, the bell jangling, as Bunny Smallbone blundered in. Billy was on his feet in an instant. "You look worn out," he said. "Here, sit down." He pulled out a chair and Bunny gratefully collapsed into it. Her hair was messy, her face was flushed.

"I'm sorry I'm so late. We've been searching and searching..." said Bunny. The look on her face told Charley they had not been successful.

"Have a sip of tea," said Charley. "Catch your breath."

Billy smiled reassuringly. "We've made some real progress with our investigations, Bunny, so don't you go giving up yet."

Bunny's face lightened a little.

"We think we know where Arthur is being held," said Charley.

"He's safe!"

"I wouldn't go as far as that," said Charley, "not yet anyway. Billy believes that Arthur is trapped inside Dr Vindicta's zoetrope."

"How is that even possible?" Bunny asked.

"With S.C.R.E.A.M. cases we deal with the impossible every week," said Billy. "I've been back to the carnival to get a closer look at the zoetrope. A terrifying device, although the mechanism is clockwork—"

"Clockwork?" said Charley.

"Yes, why?"

"Remember I was telling you about one particular

boy whose life was accidentally ruined by the Chess Club? This boy wanted to be a watchmaker, but he missed his interview for an apprenticeship because a prank got out of hand."

"Was the boy called Vindicta by any chance?" said Billy.

"No," said Charley, consulting her notes, "his name was Patrick Parker. And he was just fascinated by watches."

"Do you think this Parker might have made things for Dr Vindicta?"

"It's possible," said Charley.

"When I was checking out the tent I expected to find Dr Vindicta there," said Billy, "but instead there was a man I'd never seen before and *he* was talking with the Hobb-Hound."

"Could that be Parker?" said Charley.

"It might have been," said Billy. "Whoever he was, the idiot had made a deal with the demon."

Bunny gasped.

Charley winced. "Was there an actual contract?"

Billy nodded. "I think I found it, written around the inside of the zoetrope."

"Signed in blood, no doubt," said Charley.

All the colour faded from Bunny's face. "Why would anyone do such a thing?"

"People can get desperate, Bunny, or frustrated, or angry, and sometimes they make the terrible mistake of thinking that evil can help them."

"I don't understand," said Bunny.

"The Devil and his minions will offer you anything you want," Billy explained. "Riches, fame, revenge, you name it. But evil always wants something in return."

"What?" said Bunny. She put her teacup down. Her fingers were trembling too much to drink from it anyway.

"Your soul," said Billy.

"Isn't that just make-believe?" asked Bunny.

"I thought so too, before I joined S.C.R.E.A.M," said Charley. "But the things I've seen..." Her voice trailed away. "There is so much more to this universe than just the physical world around us."

"Heaven and Hell are real," said Billy quietly. "We don't just live this life, then turn to dust."

"So what happens to someone who loses their soul?" Bunny whispered.

"They become an empty husk, dead on the inside," said Charley, taking Bunny's hand and squeezing it between hers. "Like a shell when the living creature inside has gone."

"That's a high price to pay," said Bunny.

"The highest," Billy agreed. His eyes narrowed in thought.

"What is it?" asked Charley.

"A theory," said Billy. "This Patrick Parker that you told us about, Charley, it seems that he might have good reason to want revenge on the Chess Club."

"Absolutely," said Charley. "I can see where you're going with this."

"I can't," said Bunny.

"Well," Charley continued, "we already *think* that Parker might have built the clockwork skeleton, and we *know* that Parker has a motive to want to get his own back on the Chess Club."

"I'm still confused," said Bunny. "I thought the zoetrope belonged to Dr Vindicta?"

"Bunny," said Charley as a dazzling new revelation lit up her bright blue eyes. "You're a genius."

"I am?"

"Remember our Latin lessons?"

Bunny groaned. "Vaguely…"

"Vindicta is Latin for 'revenge'!"

"So maybe Dr Vindicta is Patrick Parker in disguise!" said Billy, rubbing his hands together with glee. "Now we're getting somewhere."

"So what next?" said Bunny.

"Well, assuming that our theory is correct, we have one more useful piece of information on our side; I know that the Hobb-Hound hasn't fulfilled its side of the bargain yet. So Parker/Vindicta's soul is safe...for now. If we're quick, we can keep it that way."

"How do you know that the contract hasn't been completed?" asked Charley.

"From the conversation I overheard, I know the name of the next boy to be kidnapped and since the Hobb-Hound only takes its victims at night, all we have to do is find the boy first, protect him from the demon, capture the demon somehow and force it to release the other boys, then find this Parker, arrest him and we can all go home for supper. Easy. Ish."

"The name?" said Charley, cutting to the chase.

"Sidney Coldblood."

"Coldblood, of course," said Charley, "the fourth member of the Chess Club!"

"Do you mean Reverend Coldblood?" asked Bunny. "My father is with him now! They're at the vicarage with Mr Fraser and Mr Hawkins."

"What are we waiting for?" said Charley.

Charley spun her wheelchair away from the table, dragging the tablecloth with her in her hurry to be away. Billy flung down a handful of change, enough for the scones and a generous tip. He was running by the time he reached the door.

# CHAPTER EIGHTEEN

# SINS OF THE FATHERS

**B**unny led the way to the vicarage, Charley easily keeping pace, her strong arms powering her chair forwards, as Billy ran alongside her. The three of them approached the front door and Billy knocked loudly. They waited but there was no reply. Billy knocked harder. "Police!" he shouted.

The door opened to reveal a short, round-bellied man.

"Yes? Can I help you, officer?"

"Reverend Coldblood?"

"Actually it's pronounced Colblud," corrected the vicar.

"Oh, all right then, that's much less sinister," said Billy. "But you *are* the Reverend Coldblood?"

"Yes, yes. What is this about?"

"We have reason to believe that your son is in great danger," said Charley.

"Sidney is safely in his bedroom," said Coldblood, pushing the door shut. "Thank you for your concern."

Billy's foot jammed the door open. "And we have some questions that we need you to answer, sir. We can either go inside and talk politely or you can accompany us to the police station and we can question you in a nice quiet cell. Which would you prefer?"

"Constable Dunstable is a personal friend of mine," said Coldblood.

"I'm very glad to hear that," said Charley, with an icy grin. "The Lord Chief Justice is a personal friend of *mine*. Shall we stop playing games and go inside now?"

Defeated, Coldblood let them in. "I have some guests with me," he said, leading the way.

"We know," said Charley. "Your friends from the 'Chess Club'. Billy, check on Sidney, I can handle this."

Billy headed straight up the stairs while Bunny helped Charley get her wheelchair up and over the front step. Major Smallbone, Mr Hawkins and Mr Fraser, the

Chess Club men, were waiting in silence, like the naughty schoolboys they used to be.

Charley entered the book-lined study with Bunny and closed the door behind her. She looked each of the men full in the eye. Only Major Smallbone had the boldness to glare back, the others dropped their gaze to the carpet.

"Gentlemen," Charley began. "I think I know why your boys have gone missing."

There was a collective gasp. "Why?" asked the major.

"Because of your silly little Chess Club," said Charley.

"I don't understand," said Hawkins. "Have our wives put you up to this? We don't drink that much, not really."

"Oh I don't mean your gambling and drinking *now*," said Charley. "I mean the foolishness you got up to when you were boys at Milverton Hall."

"What are you babbling on about?" said Major Smallbone. "That was years ago."

"Yes, it was," said Charley, "but you must ask yourselves why it was *your* boys who have been kidnapped, out of all the children in Hobb's End?"

"We've been tearing our hair out trying to work out who might have a grudge against us," said Smallbone, "but we've drawn a blank."

"You mentioned Milverton Hall," said Coldblood,

with a guilty expression. "I for one regret the cruel tricks we played when we were children. We didn't mean any harm, but looking back it can't have been funny for the other boys."

Mr Fraser glared at him. Mr Hawkins clenched his fist and gave the short fat vicar what they'd called in school a "dead arm".

"Old habits," said Hawkins with a shrug.

"I'm not proud that I once put itching powder in another boy's pants," said Coldblood, "but I've served this town wholeheartedly and, as the Bible says, once I became a man, I put away childish things."

"That's all well and good," said Charley, "but you should know that one of your so-called 'jokes' pretty much ruined someone's life."

"I can't believe that," said the major. "Good grief, the way you're talking you'd think we were the ones who'd broken the law, not the kidnapper."

"Just to be certain," said Hawkins, "is there a law against yanking someone's underpants up really hard?"

"Yes," said Charley. "That's an assault at common law."

"He made us do it," said Hawkins, pointing straight at Smallbone.

The major folded his arms across his chest. He was looking more and more like a sulky child. With a moustache. Bunny approached him. "Father, what's Charley talking about?"

"Playground games and childish pranks," he said. The moustache twitched. The cheeks went red. "We were just boys at the time. I used to think it was fun when I threw someone's cap up a tree or rolled their marbles down the drain…"

"Two counts of theft," said Charley, adding to the list of crimes.

"We were just having a bit of a laugh, weren't we, lads?" Major Smallbone looked round the room at his circle of friends, hoping for some support. He got none. "We'd tug the younger boys' trousers right down to their ankles and then kick them up the backside. We'd put spiders in their hair and flick ink on their shirts… We never meant to hurt anyone."

"But you did," said Charley. "And my investigations so far have led me to believe that one of your childhood victims has arranged to have your sons kidnapped to get his own back."

"Who?" the men asked in unison.

"Parker," said Charley.

The men looked blank. "Who?" said Fraser.

"Patrick Parker," said Charley. "He was one of your pawns. You threw his trousers over the wall and into Mr Warner's garden where he was chased by a dog."

"And you think that's reason enough for him to punish us like this?" said Hawkins.

"No, I don't," said Charley. "But what you probably didn't know is that Patrick Parker lost his apprenticeship because of your unfortunate 'joke'."

"I can see how that might make someone bitter," said Coldblood. "I think I remember Parker, but I thought he left Hobb's End years ago?"

"And now it looks like he's back," said Charley. "And we believe that he's holding your sons captive at the Carnival of Monsters." That explanation would have to do for now. This wasn't the time to start explaining about the zoetrope and the Hobb-Hound too.

"Thank goodness my Sidney is safe in his room," said Reverend Coldblood.

A head popped round the door at that moment. "He isn't," said Billy. "I've searched every room, Sidney's gone. He left this note."

*I'm fed up being treeted like a baby.
I don't care wot you say I'm going to the fair!*

# CHAPTER NINETEEN

## CARNIVAL OF MONSTERS

Charley and Billy were filling in the details for Bunny and the Chess Club as they raced to the carnival. Just like a stick in the hands of a small boy with a pocket knife, the day had been whittled away. The sun was falling fast and darkness was rising. They *had* to find Sidney before the Hobb-Hound got him.

"I think you should all prepare yourselves," said Billy. "Charley and I are not ordinary coppers, we're S.C.R.E.A.M. detectives. You might witness some things tonight that will change the way you see the world."

"What do you mean?" huffed the major, his cheeks red from running.

"The Hobb-Hound is real," said Billy. "I've seen it. It's not nice."

"How does that old legend fit in?" asked Hawkins. "I thought *Parker* had kidnapped our boys."

"He has," said Charley, "but the Hobb-Hound is helping him."

"According to the stories, the Hobb-Hound is a demon," said Coldblood, running his finger around the rim of his dog collar as if it was suddenly too tight. "How is Parker controlling a demon?"

"He isn't," said Billy. "Parker signed a contract with the Hobb-Hound, and the Hobb-Hound has the upper hand. Or should that be upper paw? Anyway, if the Hobb-Hound finds Sidney before we do, then its part of the deal will have been fulfilled. Parker's soul will be lost, and I'm afraid that your boys might be prisoners inside the zoetrope for ever."

"How could they be stuck in a contraption like that?" gasped Major Smallbone.

"Because it is so much more than just a zoetrope," Billy explained. "When the wheel spins it is magically tearing apart the fabric of reality, opening a hole between our world and another world, the dark dimension of demons. So, because the Hobb-Hound is a demon, it is free to travel *both* ways through that gate, but your son and the other boys can only move one way."

Major Smallbone shook his head in confusion. "I understand all the words you are saying, but I've no idea what you're talking about."

"All you need to know is that we are going straight to the tent with the zoetrope. That's where Parker, or Dr Vindicta or whatever he's calling himself, is holding your boys," said Billy.

"And then what?"

"Then we find a way to set all the captured boys free. If we're right, Parker will be there too and we can arrest him and make him help us. Then, together, we can find Sidney and hopefully stop the Hobb-Hound from completing the contract."

"Rescue the boys. Stop Parker. Find Sidney," said Smallbone. "Got it."

"Here we are," said Bunny, as they approached the carnival.

For Charley, the atmosphere had changed. Before she had heard screams of laughter. The carnival had been a happy place where the townsfolk of Hobb's End had gone to experience thrills and excitement. Now that she knew the dark secret at its heart, nothing about the carnival felt fun any more. Old Ted's words came back to haunt her. He'd said that the demon dogs were *drawn to fear and misery like flies to cowpats*. Was that how Parker had met the Hobb-Hound in the first place? she wondered. Had the lonely and angry boy accidentally brought the creature into his life?

"Keep your eyes skinned for Sidney," Charley ordered. "If we can find him before the Hobb-Hound gets its claws into him then that will give us half a chance. There's the tent, up ahead."

There was a queue lined up for the next performance of the Wheel of the Devil. Billy took out his official badge and pushed his way through the crowds. "Police business, move along. Nothing to see here." There was a lot of grumbling but the throng drifted away. Calmly, Charley reached her hand beneath her blanket. Her revolver was there; ready and waiting.

The tent flap was shut and Billy halted the party. "We go in on three," he whispered. "Remember to leave the talking to me and Charley. One, two, *three!*"

Billy pulled back the flap. Limelights filled the tent with an eerie green glow. Dr Vindicta was standing there beside the zoetrope, dressed in his red skullcap and cape. His forked beard and curled moustache made him appear positively fiendish.

"Police," said Billy. "We're looking for Patrick Parker."

Dr Vindicta said nothing.

The Chess Club said nothing.

There was an awkward silence in the tent.

Vindicta glowered at them from beneath his enormous black eyebrows. *If looks could kill*, thought Charley. "All of your faces are burned into my soul!" Vindicta suddenly snarled at the Chess Club, a hot fleck of spit escaping from his mouth. He whipped off his false eyebrows dramatically, wincing slightly as the gum tugged out some of his real hair. "Now remember *my* face and quiver with fear!"

Charley glanced round at the Chess Club. Their faces were blank. Vindicta ripped off his fake beard and moustache. "Your nemesis has returned!" he sneered.

"Who is this bally nincompoop?" said Major Smallbone. "I swear I've never seen him before in all my life."

With a deep sigh, Dr Vindicta took off his devilish red skullcap, pulling off his wig with it, to reveal the balding head beneath. Then he took off his red boots, each of which hid a secret heel which added nearly three inches to his height. "Now?" he said.

"Parker!" said Fraser. "Now I remember you!"

"Parker the paw—" Coldbood caught his slip of the tongue too late. He offered his hand. "I mean, *Patrick*."

Parker left Coldblood's hand hanging, staring at it with absolute disgust. Coldblood continued to try to build bridges with the man whose childhood he had made a misery. "Goodness me, we've both changed, haven't we, Patrick?" Coldblood patted his rounded stomach. "The years have flown by. How long has it been since we saw each other?"

"Twenty-one years, seven months, and six days," Parker snapped back. "Not that I've been counting."

"Look here, Parker," said Major Smallbone, "we know we made some silly 'mistakes' when we were younger, but let's all be grown up and put the past behind us, eh?"

"Mistakes?" Parker spluttered. "Mistakes! You ruined my life! Didn't any of you wonder where I went when I left school without the apprenticeship which should have been mine?"

"Not really," said Major Smallbone honestly. "Sorry."

"Sorry? *SORRY!*" Parker was shouting. "My parents were dead. Did none of you remember that either?

Didn't you wonder why I was the only one who stayed in the school boarding house through the holidays? I'm an orphan, a ward of the parish, and once my time at Milverton Hall was over I was meant to start my apprenticeship and stand on my own two feet. Only I didn't get my apprenticeship, did I? Because of YOU! And that is why I have longed to make you suffer!"

"Which is why we are here to arrest you, Mr Parker." Billy stepped forward. "I'm sorry for you, I truly am. But it would be best for everyone if you released the boys and came quietly now."

"They're the ones who should be arrested!" Parker pointed at the Chess Club.

"Taking the boys is kidnapping," said Charley. "Pure and simple. And it stops right now."

"It's their just deserts!" said Parker, a mixture of conflicting emotions crowding his face. "I wanted to end all this, but now that I'm face-to-face with these…" Parker searched for a word big enough to show quite how much he detested the Chess Club. "These *pigs!* I want them to suffer!"

Charley didn't need Billy's sixth sense to feel the waves of hatred emanating from Parker. Coolly and calmly she levelled her revolver. "You are going to release those boys, and then you are going to accompany us to the station. Justice will be done, Mr Parker."

But Parker wasn't listening. The man's face looked tortured and far more terrifying than the theatrical make-up and disguise.

Parker flicked the switch and the Grim Reaper sprung into mechanical life, winding the handle to turn the zoetrope. As if in response to Parker's anger, the tent began to shudder around them. Disturbingly it was as if someone, or some*thing*, was running around outside banging on the canvas walls trying to get to them. A wind rose from nowhere, making Parker's red cloak billow around him, and lifting the strands of hair which were scraped across his bald scalp. "Laugh at me now, Smallbone. I dare you!"

The words were angry, but Charley was struck by how afraid Parker sounded beneath the bluster and the shouting.

Charley lay her gun down and raised her hands, alarm bells ringing as she recalled the legend of the Hobb-Hound. *Beware the monster of the night, that feeds on vengeance, hate and fright.* All the fear inside the tent was exactly what the Hobb-Hound wanted!

"We're your friends, Patrick," she said kindly. "We

know that you've been wronged and we just want to help you."

For a fleeting moment Parker's furious expression dropped and Charley caught a glimpse of the once shy and gentle man beneath the anger.

Outside the tent, something growled.

"Stay calm," Charley urged. But even as she said it, she had to fight against her own rising fear.

The zoetrope was spinning madly, revealing the silhouettes of the kidnapped boys trapped inside. Major Smallbone drew Bunny close and raised his voice. "We're sorry, damn it! Now release our boys!"

The Reverend Coldblood dropped to his knees and began to pray.

"Don't do this," said Billy, goosebumps blistering his hands. "I'm begging you!"

"Beg all you like, Mr Policeman, but nothing in the world can stop me now!"

# CHAPTER TWENTY

# OLD DOG, NEW TRICKS

The wheel spun faster and faster. The images flickered before their eyes. The boys. The lost boys. Arthur Smallbone, Fred Hawkins, Herbert Fraser. Running. Running for their lives.

What the Chess Club had done was wrong and Billy hated bullies, but he'd done some stupid things when he was a kid – like putting salt in the sugar bowl and laughing himself silly when his older brothers choked on their tea. Major Smallbone and the others never considered the consequences of their jokes and Billy supposed that was the lesson they were learning now.

But the price that they were having to pay was too high. Parker was the bully now, even though he still felt like the victim.

Billy felt especially sorry for Arthur, Fred and Herbert. No matter what their fathers had done when they were young, these boys hadn't hurt Patrick Parker. Yet their punishment inside the zoetrope was a hundred times more frightening than what Parker had been forced to endure.

The wheel was revolving so quickly now that it was just a blur. The wind that it was creating was so strong that Billy had to lean into it to prevent himself from being knocked down. Billy glanced at Parker, so scared and small, in spite of the anger he had shown.

Sparks of magical energy arced and flashed above the zoetrope, as fierce as a thunderstorm, lighting up the tent. The flashes were so bright that they left Billy blinking, but he could still see a huge dark shadow stalking around the outside of the tent. *A hound-shaped shadow.*

Suddenly, the beast's claws tore a hole in one canvas wall and, with a monstrous howl, the Hobb-Hound burst into the tent. The demon dog studied them each in turn, as if it was seeing which one to pick off first, and even

Major Smallbone – a big man, a soldier who had seen the horror of battle – flinched and cowered beneath the intensity of those burning red eyes.

"Good God, no!" said the Reverend Coldblood, his face illuminated by the ghastly red light of the Hobb-Hound's gaze.

"You are all so afraid of me," the Hobb-Hound mocked. The demon rose up on its hind legs. It seemed to be growing by the second. It wasn't the sort of dog you would want to stroke if you enjoyed having fingers, Billy thought. This was a guard dog straight from Hell!

Then the Hobb-Hound threw back its massive head and gave a barking laugh. "And Parker is most afraid of all!"

Billy spotted Parker at the side of the tent, his hands pressed to the sides of his face. A scream escaped from Parker's lips; anger mixed with terror.

And still the zoetrope spun. Faster and faster. Billy knew that he had seconds to act. Hanging on to a tent pole to keep himself from being knocked down by the whirlwind, Billy rummaged in his satchel. As a S.C.R.E.A.M. detective he didn't go into situations like this unprepared. After a few seconds of blind fumbling, his fingers closed around a small glass bottle. This should teach it a lesson!

"We're sorry, Parker!" Major Smallbone shouted, trying to make his voice heard above the whirlwind. "Truly, truly sorry!"

"Please forgive us," yelled Fraser, crawling to Parker on his hands and knees. "I'm begging you!"

Something about those words reignited Parker's fury. "Do you remember when I begged for *you* to stop?" said Parker. "What did you do to me?"

"Laughed and threw your trousers over the wall and into old Walnut's garden," Hawkins confessed, shamefaced.

"Exactly!" Parker shouted madly. "Who's laughing now?"

Just then Billy brought the bottle to his mouth. Grabbing the cork between his teeth, he pulled the stopper out and then hurled the bottle at the monster, like a cricketer aiming for the stumps.

"Holy water grenade!" said Billy with satisfaction as he watched it fly towards the Hobb-Hound. Bullseye!

The bottle shattered on the demon's chest and the contents of the missile quickly went to work. There was a smell like burning hair and the Hobb-Hound yelped in pain, its head thrashing from side to side.

The holy water sizzled and bubbled as it wounded the demon.

But the effect didn't last long.

Billy only had one more bomb and he knew that he had to make it count. *If I can get it right between the eyes...*

He took careful aim, but unfortunately, just as Billy was releasing the missile, Parker grabbed at his arm, ruining the shot. The bottle sailed over the demon and fell harmlessly to the floor of the tent, spilling its precious contents in the dust.

"You idiot!" snapped Billy.

"My turn!" said Charley, holding her gun in both hands. She squinted down the barrel and took aim, doing her best to compensate for the storm which howled around them. Then she squeezed the trigger three times in rapid succession. *BANG. BANG. BANG.*

They weren't just any old bullets either. Luther Sparkwell, their boss in S.C.R.E.A.M., had handcrafted them himself. They were made of pure silver as a defence against werewolves. They contained a glass vial in their core, filled with a mix of garlic and hawthorn – deadly to vampires. They were engraved with ancient blessings; words of great power that had been hidden in the secret texts of the long-lost library of Alexandria – enough to shrivel most demons to a crisp. To put it bluntly, these bullets packed a punch.

But only if they hit the target.

The dog's head whipped round but before Charley's shots could strike home, its huge bat wings swung out like a shield. Although the demon seemed to be made of flesh and blood, the wings were as strong as iron. The bullets struck with a *clang!* which echoed through the tent, and then ricocheted away.

"Damn!" said Charley, snapping off her last two shots. One high, to the head, one low to the legs – only for the impenetrable shield of the bat wings to deflect them again.

Major Smallbone flung himself to the ground as a bullet zinged in his direction and pierced a hole in the tent. "Parker, please! We're sorry. We really are. Please call off your dog!"

Billy saw the change come over Parker. It was as if someone had poured a bucket of cold water over his head. The hot anger which had consumed him began to fizzle out as reality dawned. Perhaps it was the sincerity in Major Smallbone's voice that touched him? Perhaps it was the bullet that had narrowly missed Parker's head? Most probably it was the reality of what he had got himself into. Because Parker knew that once this foul creature had captured Sidney Coldblood, those two red eyes would be hunting for him.

"Please save us, Patrick," said Fraser, on his hands and knees. "Please make it stop."

"Please," said Hawkins.

"Please," said Coldblood.

"Please," said Smallbone. "If not for us, then for our children."

"He can't." The Hobb-Hound laughed. "We made a deal. I capture the children for him, he gives me his immortal soul."

"The deal is off," said Parker defiantly. "I've changed my mind!"

"We have a contract," said the Hobb-Hound, "which you were very happy to sign."

"That was a long time ago," Parker protested.

"YOU SIGNED," boomed the Hobb-Hound, "IN HOT BLOOD! And tonight, when Sidney *Coldblood* is imprisoned in the zoetrope with those other brats, I shall claim my payment in FULL!" The Hobb-Hound's jaws slavered. "Souls as scared as yours are so tasty, Parker," said the Hobb-Hound, licking its black lips.

The demon's baleful eyes swept the tent like two red

lanterns, then with one slash of its mighty wings it ripped another hole in the battered tent and flapped away into the sky.

One second later the screaming started.

# CHAPTER TWENTY-ONE

## WHO LET THE DEMON DOG OUT?

Charley and Billy were first outside the tent.

"It's pandemonium," said Charley, calmly slipping five more rounds into her revolver. Every which way they turned there was panic at the Carnival of Monsters. Nobody was enjoying being scared any more; they were petrified for real.

The Hobb-Hound had launched itself into the sky with a bone-rattling howl and everyone – parents, children, young couples, old couples, *everyone* – was tripping over themselves in the mad rush to get away. The clowns especially were tripping over themselves.

Enormous comedy shoes are always a disadvantage when you are running for your life.

The Hobb-Hound flew up higher and higher until it was just a hideous black shape against the blind white eye of the moon. Then it dived, with another terrifying howl.

Parker, Bunny and the Chess Club stumbled out of the tent. "Look at what you've done!" bellowed Major Smallbone as he took in the scene of chaos. He grabbed Parker and shook him by the shoulders. "Look!"

"I never meant for any of this to happen," said Parker. "I just wanted to get my own back."

"Stop it, boys!" Charley ordered, making her point absolutely crystal clear by raising her revolver and shooting into the sky. The men stopped.

"Our canine friend is going to claim your soul, Mr Parker," said Charley. She raised her finger like a schoolteacher. "Unless we can stop it, of course."

Parker was desperate. "Tell us what we have to do."

Billy stepped in. "Coldblood, you and I have got to find Sidney. If we can get to him before the Hobb-Hound that should give us the upper hand, but I'm afraid the Hobb-Hound is getting stronger by the second."

"I've noticed that too," said Charley. "As Old Ted said, it feeds on fear."

"Then this must be a five-course banquet," said Major Smallbone angrily. The Hobb-Hound swooped low over the carnival, scattering the crowd in all directions like frightened rabbits.

"With after dinner mints, too," said Billy, grabbing Coldblood's arm and heading off with him in search of Sidney.

"Wait!" said Bunny, making to follow them, but Charley stopped her, grabbing her sleeve.

"No, I'm going to need the rest of you to help me if we are going to stand a chance of stopping this demon once and for all," said Charley.

"What do you need us to do?" said Major Smallbone.

"I need you to do as you're told. Parker, lead the way to the Minotaur's Maze of Mirrors. Quick!"

"This is hardly the time for—" Fraser began.

"Hush!" Charley tutted. "What did I say?"

Fraser dropped his head obediently.

"You're *my* pawns now," said Charley with a grin as they raced on through the fair.


"SIDNEY!" the Reverend Coldblood shouted at the top of his voice, trying to make himself heard above the shouts and yells of the crowd. Billy and Coldblood were fighting against the stream, being buffeted and elbowed on every side as they headed *towards* the Hobb-Hound, not away from it.

The Hobb-Hound was rampaging through the Carnival of Monsters with glee; barking, snarling, drooling, red eyes ablaze. First it bounded on all fours, then it swooped through the air. Several of the tents had already been flattened, knocked down by a swing of its tail or a swipe of its wing.

Billy ran towards the helter-skelter and the steam-powered rides; he had a vague idea about climbing up to get a better chance of spotting Sidney. A stallholder dressed as an Egyptian mummy blundered into Billy, spinning him round. Billy did a double take. The last time he'd met a mummy he had almost ended up as one!

"SIDNEY!" Billy called. "*SIDNEY!*"

By his side, Coldblood was at his wits' end. "My poor boy," he said. "Where are you, Sidney?"

The carnival was emptying now. There was nothing like a monster on the loose to make people suddenly fancy an early night. But still there was no sign of Sidney. Billy's head whipped back and forth – the boy could be anywhere. Hiding inside one of the tents, under one of the stalls, off in the woods. *Anywhere.*

The one thing that convinced Billy that Sidney *had* to be nearby was the fact the Hobb-Hound was circling overhead. The demon had been able to find the other boys, and Billy had no doubt that the Hobb-Hound *would* find its prey. If the Hobb-Hound was here, then Sidney was too...but where?

Billy's eyes were drawn to the big wheel. It was stationary now, the carriages swinging. The last remaining passengers were clambering over the sides; risking broken arms and legs, they scrambled down the wheel as if it was a giant climbing frame. There was one carriage, however, where a passenger was trapped and panicking. Right at the top of the wheel, at the highest point, a boy was crying for help.

"SIDNEY!" Coldblood shouted.

The boy stood up and waved vigorously, making the carriage rock violently back and forth.

"Help me, Pa!"

"I'm coming!" said Billy, racing towards the Ferris wheel.

In the sky, the Hobb-Hound howled in triumph, and circled around, heading straight for the big wheel. Straight for the helpless Sidney.

Billy ran like he had never run before. The race was on!

He leaped over the remains of the candyfloss stall, dodged a falling tent pole, skidded round the Coconut Shy of Doom, tripped over a guy rope, grazed his knee, clambered back to his feet and kept on running. He reached the Ferris wheel before the demon – just.

Unfortunately it was only *one second* before the demon. And Billy was at the bottom of the wheel, whilst the demon was at the top.

Billy began to climb, hand over hand.

"Hide under the seat, Sidney!" Billy shouted. "Don't let it get you!"

"Brilliant!" Sidney shouted back sarcastically. "I'd never have thought of that."

Billy bit his lip – *kids* – and kept climbing.

The Hobb-Hound landed on the top of the wheel, and Billy heard the structure groan beneath the creature's weight. The big wheel was made of wood and steel – it was not made to withstand an assault by a monster.

Fortunately, Sidney was taking Billy's advice and he wasn't making it easy for the Hobb-Hound. Billy was climbing through a rain of splinters and wood chippings as the demon ripped the fragile carriage apart to get to the frightened boy.

Billy ducked as a length of plank spun by, inches from his face. He could hear Sidney whimpering as the demon got closer. The climbing was difficult, but difficult was all in a day's work for S.C.R.E.A.M.

Billy had been clambering up the Ferris wheel as if it was a giant spider's web, using the spokes of the wheel as a climbing frame. Now he was nearly at the top and he inched his way out towards the rim, the wooden circle which supported all the swinging carriages – or what was left of them anyway. Suddenly Billy felt vulnerable. The ground was a long way down and the Hobb-Hound was far too near. Oh, and the Ferris wheel was so badly damaged it might collapse at any moment. Apart from that, he was fine.

The Hobb-Hound was perched directly above Sidney's carriage and distracted by the prospect of his next victim… *Which is lucky for me, but not so lucky for Sidney*, thought Billy, as he inched ever closer. Not daring to look down, Billy scrambled up so that he was sitting on the outer rim of the Ferris wheel, gripping with his thighs as well as his hands. He needed to buy himself some time to get Sidney away from the Hobb-Hound. But how? His knees were trembling even as his mind was racing.

The holy water bomb hadn't worked, but Billy had a few other tricks up his sleeve, or in his satchel to be precise. He had a bone for one thing…and didn't all dogs love a good bone? Billy grinned as the plan began to form. This wasn't just any bone, it was the finger bone of a saint, inscribed with a powerful prayer, engraved by the blind monks of the mountaintop monastery of Monte Cassino. Billy's idea was simple enough – throw the bone, hope that the Hobb-Hound caught it in its mouth and double hope that the holy bone would make it choke. Surely something so holy would be like poison to the demon? Then, while the Hobb-Hound was distracted, Billy would rescue Sidney. What could possibly go wrong?

Billy rummaged in his bag and found the bone. Taking it out, it seemed disappointingly small when Billy compared it with the Hobb-Hound's slathering mouth. He was about to scrap that plan when he remembered the coconut he had won on his first visit to the carnival. Gripping as tightly as he could with his legs, Billy found some string in his satchel and tied the holy bone to the coconut as best he could, leaving him with a rugby ball shaped missile to throw. Of course, it still might not be enough to block the Hobb-Hound's monstrous jaws, but it was worth a try.

Up close, the demon was even more terrifying, but Billy refused to let fear get the better of him. He bit his lip and kept going, shuffling his way along the beam to get to Sidney, clasping the wood tightly with his hands and thighs; hanging on for grim death.

There was almost nothing left of the carriage now. Billy was amazed it was still hanging there. He could see Sidney cowering beneath the shattered remains of the seat. The Hobb-Hound was crouched over him, long trails of drool spilling from its lips in anticipation. It was taking its time, Billy realized, like a cat tormenting a terrified mouse. Sidney was whimpering and the Hobb-Hound was enjoying the taste of the boy's delicious fear.

"Oi!" shouted Billy. The Hobb-Hound's neck whip-cracked towards him, and Billy felt the force of its baleful red eyes. He held his missile up and saw the Hobb-Hound's nostrils flare as it picked up the scent of the bone. *This just might work...*

"Din-dins," said Billy. "You want this, don't you?"

The Hobb-Hound growled like thunder. Its black lips curled back to reveal teeth that could reduce Billy to mincemeat.

"Good doggie," said Billy, feeling less certain about this plan already.

The Hobb-Hound's eyes narrowed. Billy could see its leg muscles tensing, ready to pounce on him and grab the bone. Or possibly bite his head off.

"STAY!" shouted Billy. He locked his eyes on Sidney, who was still cowering beneath the seat. "Sidney, look at me!" The boy looked. "I'm coming for you."

The Hobb-Hound barked savagely.

Billy knew he would only get one shot at this. He deliberately tossed his missile *over* Sidney…and the Hobb-Hound went for it, snatching it out of the air with a mighty *SNAP*! Billy knew that he had bought a few seconds at most. He stretched out his hand: "Come to me, Sidney!"

Sidney Coldblood went rigid.

"Hurry!" Billy urged.

Still the frightened boy didn't budge.

Meanwhile the dog demon was coughing and retching. The coconut was big enough to wedge the creature's jaws open, and the holy bone was like acid in the Hobb-Hound's mouth. Billy could actually see foam bubbling and frothing from its lips, as the pure good of the saint's bone met the pure evil of the Hobb-Hound.

Billy inched closer, the sinews in his arm aching as he stretched as far as he could… "Sidney, give me your hand!

*Nearly there.*

Too late!

With a bark of triumph the Hobb-Hound dislodged the bone. A sweep of its wing almost knocked Billy off the Ferris wheel, and while Billy struggled to regain his grip, the Hobb-Hound turned its attention back to Sidney with renewed savagery. The black claws tore the last fragments of the seat apart and grabbed Sidney by the shoulders. With a howl of victory, the Hobb-Hound flapped its wings and took off, with Sidney Coldblood in its clutches.

*I hope I live to regret this*, thought Billy, as he stood up precariously and launched himself into the air after Sidney. *Or it's going to be the shortest rescue attempt in history!*

# CHAPTER TWENTY-TWO

## GIVE A DOG A BONE

Charley was moving quickly. Now that the men had got over the shock of taking orders from a girl, things were progressing well. Although he had seemed as daft as a ferret when she met him, it turned out that Old Ted really knew his stuff. He had been right about the Hobb-Hound being drawn to fear, and he might well be right about the demon being driven off, or least deterred, by light.

Of course, she might be wrong. Best not to think about that really, because she didn't have a backup plan.

"No," Charley ordered, with as much patience as she

could manage. "Not there – *there*. It is essential that the mirrors make a perfect circle."

"They *are* rather heavy," puffed Fraser as he struggled to carry one of the enormous fairground mirrors. The Chess Club had lugged them over from the Maze of the Minotaur and now they were repositioning them in the same huge tent which housed the monstrous zoetrope. "I don't want to put my back out."

"I am rescuing *your* children from a demon," she shot back.

"All right then, where do you want it?" said Fraser meekly.

"Left a bit," said Charley, directing the whole operation. "There! Perfect." She admired her handiwork – a circle of mirrors now stood beside the zoetrope. Viewed from above, it would have looked like a figure 8. This would work, Charley was certain of it. Well, ninety-eight per cent certain. Perhaps ninety-two. Certainly no lower than eighty-seven. All that she needed for her plan to succeed was for the Hobb-Hound to stand in exactly the right spot, in the centre of the circle of mirrors.

The men were sprawled around the tent, breathing heavily from their physical exertions. Charley clapped her hands to rouse them. "Right, I need every limelight and lantern that you can get your hands on. Quickly now, spit-spot."

Major Smallbone, Fraser, Hawkins and Parker all climbed to their feet. "Anything else?"

"Gunpowder would be amazing."

"The human cannonball," said Parker. "Follow me."

"Not so fast," said Charley.

Parker stopped. "Don't you want me to show them the way?"

"It's an enormous cannon sticking up into the sky. How hard can it be to find? No," said Charley. "I've got a special job for you, Mr Parker. Do the words 'human bait' mean anything to you?"

# CHAPTER TWENTY-THREE

## FULL MOON

Billy had made some stupid mistakes before, but this one was a prizewinner.

The Hobb-Hound was flying away, carrying Sidney Coldblood in its claws. The boy was hanging beneath the demon like a mouse carried away by an owl. A really massive evil owl.

Billy had jumped off the top of the Ferris wheel, hoping to grab Sidney. Perhaps together they could force the Hobb-Hound closer to the ground and make it release the boy.

But Billy had missed Sidney's outstretched hand.

He had missed Sidney's flapping jacket.

He had missed the Hobb-Hound altogether.

What Billy *had* managed to grab was Sidney's trousers. Right at the ankles.

And now two terrible things were happening. Firstly, Sidney was being carried higher and higher into the night sky, with Billy clinging to his trousers for dear life. And secondly, Billy's weight on Sidney's trousers was steadily pulling them off, bringing his underpants down too. Sidney was mute with terror. The poor boy was being carried away by a shadow demon, and, as an added indignity, anyone looking up would get a perfect view of Sidney's smooth pink backside.

Billy had assumed that the Hobb-Hound would drag Sidney straight to its prison – the zoetrope. However, it seemed that the creature had other ideas. The mighty demon was circling the carnival and giving no indication that it would come in to land soon. Billy gritted his teeth in determination. Each downdraught of the demon's bat wings threatened to knock him off, each squirm from Sidney Coldblood caused the boy's trousers to sink lower.

Billy's fingers were screaming with the effort of holding on, but Sidney's trousers were too slippery. Billy feared that he was only delaying the inevitable.

The Hobb-Hound must have sensed it too. It began to swoop and twirl through the air, looping round and round, diving and rolling in a vicious attempt to shake Billy loose.

It worked.

Billy fell.

Charley looked Patrick Parker in the eye.

"I can't blame you for wanting to get your own back on this lot." Smallbone, Fraser and Hawkins all looked suitably ashamed of themselves. "But you got yourself into this mess, Patrick, and so now you've got to get yourself out of it."

Parker looked as if he was about to burst into tears. "But you want me to be some sort of carrot!" he blustered. "Something that you can dangle in front of the Hobb-Hound to make it chase after me."

"More like a bone than a carrot," said Hawkins.

"You're not helping," snapped Charley. "Yes," she addressed Parker again, speaking in calm measured tones so as not to scare him any more than she already had. "I want you to be the bo—" Charley caught herself slightly too late. "To be the *bold* hero of the night."

She turned towards the Chess Club. "You boys can all run along now," she said. "I've given you the shopping list."

Fraser, Hawkins and Major Smallbone all trooped out at the double; only Bunny stayed back. "Do you want me to keep polishing these mirrors, Charley?"

"Please. We need them to be as reflective as possible."

Bunny had a cloth, torn from her own dress. As she busied herself cleaning the distorting mirrors, her own reflection stared back at her, making her face as thin as a beanpole one moment, then as fat as a balloon the next.

Parker was so terrified, he was actually trembling while he was polishing. "I've always been fearful…that's probably why they picked on me in the first place."

"Stop that," said Charley. "We don't have time to waste on self-pity. They picked on you because *they* were weak, not you. Bullies are the worst sort of cowards in my book. Now, blow your nose, Mr Parker, and we'll go through the plan one more time."

For the second time that day Billy Flint was flying through the air. Only this time he didn't have the promise of a nice, safe net to catch him. Oh, and he was flying straight down. More plummeting really.

Billy should have panicked. He should have screamed his lungs out. But what was the point? There was nothing that he could do to change the situation. His clothes flapped around him as he nosedived towards the ground. He shut his eyes, and hoped it wouldn't hurt too much.

He'd heard that your life flashes before your eyes when you are about to die. Billy didn't see his *whole* life; there probably wasn't enough time for that. But he did see Charley's face – she looked furious! He could hear her voice too, inside his head. *Billy Flint! Of all the foolish, irresponsible ways to go, you had to choose this?*

But when the impact came, the ground was surprisingly soft, and as all of Billy's limbs *weren't* instantly shattered, he dared to open his eyes. What the...? He was bouncing back up again!

By some miracle Billy had landed on top of one of the carnival tents and it had cushioned his fall! He bounced twice more, a smaller rebound each time, and then finally came to a rest. Although his heart was beating hard enough to box its way out of his ribcage, Billy Flint was alive! He wanted to punch the air with sheer relief, but his arms were trembling too much. Instead he lowered himself off the roof of the marquee and slid to the ground. He actually pressed his face into the dewy grass and kissed it. He had never been more grateful.

Billy was very aware that his escape might be short-lived, though. The Hobb-Hound was still circling. Billy watched as the demon landed on the top of the helter-skelter. Poor Sidney Coldblood was helpless to resist as the Hobb-Hound enfolded the boy in its wings. To Billy's horror the demon's jaws started to salivate, until long globules of ectoplasmic drool poured from its mouth and onto Sidney, trapping the boy in a deadly embrace.

It was just as Charley had described in her experiment with the litmus paper – the Hobb-Hound's saliva was changing Sidney with every gelatinous drip. Billy knew that even if he lived to be a hundred, which was highly unlikely in his line of work, he would never forget the bubbling, slurping, belching sounds as a waterfall of drool drenched Sidney from head to foot.

The Hobb-Hound wasn't *eating* Sidney, it was using the supernatural properties of its saliva to *change* the boy. Drop by drop, glop by shlop, Sidney Coldblood the boy was melting into Sidney Coldblood the living shadow. It was terrible to see the boy's transformation from flesh and blood to insubstantial mist! Finally, Sidney simply disappeared, blinking out of earthly existence. No doubt the zoetrope was spinning right now, opening up the dimensional gateway and trapping Sidney's shadow inside with the other boys.

Its grisly work finished, the Hobb-Hound shook its head, sending the last dollops of drool flying from its wobbling chops. Then it stretched its bat wings wide in victory and howled at the moon. The Hobb-Hound had fulfilled its part of the bargain by capturing all four boys. Now it wanted payment. A soul.

"Parker!" the Hobb-Hound spoke in a growl, loud enough to be heard through the abandoned carnival. "Come out, come out, wherever you are!"

# CHAPTER TWENTY-FOUR

## SCREAM IF YOU WANT TO GO FASTER

**B**illy sprinted through the debris of the Carnival of Monsters. The Reverend Coldblood had been following Sidney and the Hobb-Hound from the ground and was running after Billy, wheezing and puffing. Billy made straight for the zoetrope. This was where the case was going to end. One way or another.

He was heading into the marquee when he bumped into Parker coming out. "Whoa there, sunshine," said Billy. "Where do you think you're going?"

"Charley says she needs more time to prepare the trap."

Charley's voice called from inside the tent. She sounded under pressure. "I'm not ready, Billy! I need another four or five minutes to lay the fuse wire."

"Four or five minutes of trap-building time coming right up, Duchess!" He turned to Parker. "I hope you're feeling fit, because we've got to lead the Hobb-Hound on a wild goose chase."

"I know, I know," said Parker reluctantly, "and we're the geese."

"Better than being a chicken though," said Billy with an encouraging smile. "Come on, mate." Billy made a quick check of the skyline. The Hobb-Hound wasn't perched on the helter-skelter any more. So where was it?

As fast as they could, Billy and Parker ran between the tents, ducking and weaving through the wreckage of ruined sideshows. "We could coax it towards the carousel," suggested Parker. "That's about as far away from the zoetrope as we can get."

The carousel was stationary, the skeletal horses frozen in mid-gallop. Billy and Parker sprinted towards it. The structure had a few advantages, Billy thought. There was a solid roof to protect them from an overhead assault, the sides were open so they could see the Hobb-Hound coming no matter which direction it approached from, and there were lots of wooden horses to hide behind. It only had to work for a short time, Billy reminded himself.

But where was the Hobb-Hound? He needed the demon dog to focus on him and Parker, not Charley and the zoetrope.

"Here, doggie, doggie, doggie!"

Billy heard a growl much closer than he had expected and looked up. The demon was directly overhead! A fat, wet drop of something slimy splatted onto Billy's shoulder. He flicked the disgusting liquid away and anxiously examined the tips of his fingers which were sticky with drool. They were still there, thank God! *I'm not going to be a dog's dinner today!*

"Quick!" said Billy, as he and Parker scrambled up onto the ride. "How do you start this thing?"

"Why would you want to do that?" spluttered Parker.

"We've got to keep it distracted," said Billy. The ground shook as the Hobb-Hound landed behind them. It was as big as a bull now; growing fatter and stronger by the moment as it feasted on the fear it had spread. It started stalking their way, its massive dog head low to the ground, wings swept back, tail tall and straight. The glowing red eyes cast beams like lanterns, searching in the dark. "Don't argue, Parker. Just do it!"

Fortunately the carousel's coal furnace hadn't died down, and so when Parker pulled the lever the steam engine chugged into life. A pipe organ began to play a ghostly tune. *Brilliant,* thought Billy. *Music to be hunted by.*

All around him the skeleton horses started to move, up and down, up and down. The whole carousel was turning, slowly at first, but getting quicker.

The Hobb-Hound leaped onto the carousel and began to slash a path through the wooden horses towards them. Its black talons were incredibly sharp. A horse's head went bouncing away with a single swipe. Instinctively Billy's hand touched his own neck. "This way!"

Half-running, half-crawling, Billy and Parker scrambled away from the advancing demon.

It was hard going. The rise and fall of the horses and the movement of the carousel combined to give Billy a seasick feeling in his guts. Everything was made a hundred times worse by the Hobb-Hound, which was only a few paces behind, ripping its way through the entire herd of skeleton horses.

"Please run," the Hobb-Hound growled with merciless humour. "It makes this so much fun!"

They had gone full circle and arrived back at the

control lever. Billy yanked on it with both hands, pulling it down until it was level with the floor.

"What are you doing?" gasped Parker. "The ride isn't meant to go that fast. If the engine gets too hot there might be an explosion!"

"Wouldn't that be brilliant!" said Billy as he steered Parker to the very edge of the carousel. "Now JUMP!"

Billy and Parker landed together in an awkward heap; they would have bruises but no broken bones. The carousel was shuddering as it spun dangerously fast and they staggered away to a safe distance, in case it really did blow up. Looking back, Billy saw that the Hobb-Hound was wedged in somehow, trapped by its massive bulk and unable to get free from the runaway ride.

The slow and spooky music was going faster too. It sounded ridiculous now and Billy couldn't help but smile. "Well done, Parker," said Billy, giving the man a nudge. "The carousel was a great idea of yours."

There was a deafening bang as the engine exploded and, with a cloud of steam, the carousel quivered to a halt. On shaky legs the Hobb-Hound disentangled itself from the twisted wreckage, stumbling and wobbling like a newborn horse. "We had a deal, Parker. Your soul for the boys," it snarled. Then it did a sort of hiccupping burp. Billy was reminded of a cat coughing up a furball and the image was completed when the Hobb-Hound lowered its head and was violently sick in the grass. Apparently demons could get dizzy!

When it had finished, the Hobb-Hound growled and fixed them both in a hateful stare. Billy started to run first, towing Parker behind him.

"Ready or not, Charley, here we come!"

# CHAPTER TWENTY-FIVE

## TRAPPED!

**B**illy didn't know how he and Parker made it back to the tent alive, but they did. It was surprising just how fast they could run with the right motivation. Like being chased by an enormous soul-eating demon dog, for example.

Billy's lungs were burning and his back was slick with sweat as he and Parker burst into the tent.

"Six minutes, thirty-seven seconds," said Charley looking at her watch.

"I like what you've done with the place," said Billy, catching his breath. "You've got mirrors underneath those torn curtains, I guess?"

Charley nodded. "I've arranged the circle of mirrors to maximize the intensity of the light – I think that's our best weapon against the Hobb-Hound."

Billy frowned. The tent was dimly lit by a single yellow limelight. "We're going to need a bigger lamp."

Charley smiled. "Don't worry, Billy. I've got that covered."

"And where are the others? They haven't left us to it, have they?"

"We're here!" called Bunny. Billy saw her hand waving from behind one of the mirrors. "We're waiting for Charley to give the signal!"

"I love a good trap," said Billy approvingly.

Standing silently beside Billy, Parker seemed exhausted. "I'd better take up my position then," he said, quivering like a jelly as he made his way into the centre of the circle of mirrors.

"There isn't any other way," said Charley. "I wish there was."

"Like a lamb to the slaughter," whispered Hawkins, loud enough to fill the tent.

"That isn't helping," said Charley, retreating from the circle and taking her place behind the mirrors.

"I'm so afraid," said Parker.

"Chin up," said Billy, joining Parker in the danger zone. "You didn't think we would let you do this alone, did you?"

But Parker didn't have time to answer. With a fearsome snarl, the Hobb-Hound burst into the tent, catching Billy unawares and sending him sprawling to the ground, face down.

Billy was pinned to the floor, with the Hobb-Hound's huge front paws crushing his shoulders. He kicked and thrashed, but it was no good. The Hobb-Hound was huge and it wasn't budging.

A fat string of drool landed on Billy's naked neck. He wondered how much of the foul stuff it would take for him to be dissolved, only to reappear in the shadow prison. A ghastly wet tongue lay a trail through Billy's hair. He wouldn't have to wait long to find out.

Billy could feel the oxygen being squeezed from his lungs as the Hobb-Hound's weight threatened to squash him flat. His face was pressed into the grass, one eye closed. But with his other eye he could see Patrick Parker sitting on his bottom, his arms wrapped tightly round his knees.

"Leave him alone," said Parker. "It's me you want."

Just as Billy thought his ribcage was about to crack,

the Hobb-Hound lifted its paws and swatted him to one side; a discarded toy.

Now the demon turned all its attention to Parker. Its black tongue licked its slavering lips in anticipation of a nice juicy soul. The dreadful red eyes flared. Its tail wagged from side to side.

"Say goodbye to your soul, Patrick Parker," snarled the Hobb-Hound. "It belongs to me."

"Not if I have anything to do with it!" said Charley. "NOW!"

Billy scrambled away on his hands and knees as Charley's trap sprang into action. All around the circle, the Chess Club whipped off the canvas sheets to reveal the mirrors underneath. Bunny heaved the last mirror into place, closing the circle completely around the demon. The Hobb-Hound seemed startled and, for a moment, took its attention off Parker. It swung its huge head left and right. Whichever way it turned, dozens of pairs of red eyes glared back at it. The Hobb-Hound saw that it was *surrounded* by demons, each one more twisted and distorted than the last, reflected by the fairground mirrors. It flicked its tail in agitation and started to pace like a caged animal.

At the back of his mind Billy was aware of a hissing

sound. It was as if a dozen rattlesnakes had been released. But they weren't snakes. Billy guessed what was coming next and raised his hand to shield his eyes.

All around the circle of mirrors, every limelight from the entire carnival suddenly blazed a brilliant white. The hissing sound had been the oxyhydrogen flames firing up, Billy realized, no doubt lit by Charley. The effect was instant…and devastating. *Very Charley*, thought Billy. *Dangerous science!* In a flash, the night-time gloom of the tent became the dazzling light of the midday sun.

Beam after beam of light struck the Hobb-Hound, like silver swords. The light pierced the darkness…it also pierced the Hobb-Hound!

The demon began to scream, as the intense shafts of light struck it from every angle. The Hobb-Hound tried to protect itself, drawing its wings around its body like a shield, but the light burned through. Billy remembered once using a magnifying glass to focus the sun's rays so that he could burn his name on his desk; the effect on the Hobb-Hound was much the same. Its wings were pierced time and again and the air inside the tent was filled with the smell of smoky bacon.

"Bunny!" Charley called. "Round two. You do the honours."

Bunny emerged from behind the mirror wall with her own lighted taper in her hand. "This is for hurting my brother," she said, as she bent down and lit the ring of gunpowder.

With a *crackle* and a *fizz* the light inside the circle of mirrors became even more intense. The Hobb-Hound was in deep distress now. It yelped like a puppy. It had nowhere to run, no defence. Its black fur started to smoulder and as its power started to fade the demon began to shrink.

"Let there be light," breathed Billy, a smile forming at the corners of his mouth.

Then the Hobb-Hound lashed out with its mighty claws, smashing one mirror into a thousand shards. Its wings were full of holes, but the tips were still as strong as steel and it sliced another mirror in two. Then another and another, until the splinters covered the floor of the tent like diamonds. The ring of gunpowder burned itself out. The light began to dim again.

"Is that all you've got?" screamed the beast.

# CHAPTER TWENTY-SIX

## BAD DOG

The mirrors were broken. The light was dying. The Hobb-Hound was growing back to its full size. All they could do was watch. Coldblood was praying under his breath. Bunny drew close to her father, who put his arm protectively around her shoulders. Fraser drew close to Hawkins, who put *his* arm around Fraser's shoulders. Parker was silent, presumably waiting for his fate.

The Hobb-Hound rose up onto its hind feet. "You thought you could destroy me with some torches?" The demon began to laugh.

The Grim Reaper twitched and began to turn the handle which spun the zoetrope of its own accord. Round and round it spun, and there were the lost boys – Arthur Smallbone, Fred Hawkins, Herbert Fraser and now Sidney Coldblood – running and running and running in the endless circle of their prison.

The Hobb-Hound snarled. It was a bone-chilling sound and even Billy took a step back.

"You are all terrified of me, aren't you?" mocked the demon.

The Chess Men were silent.

The Hobb-Hound began to laugh, stalking towards Parker and looming over him. "Be afraid!" it boomed. "Be *very* afraid!"

"I am not afraid of you," said Charley Steel.

The Hobb-Hound's head snapped round. "What?"

Louder this time, she shouted back. "I am not afraid of you!"

"You should be," barked the Hobb-Hound.

"Billy! Bunny!" encouraged Charley.

"I'm not afraid of you either," shouted Billy, catching Charley's drift. If the light hadn't been enough to defeat this demon, perhaps they could still *starve* it to death… If they could summon enough courage between them.

"I'm not afraid of you!" yelled Bunny.

The Hobb-Hound blinked.

"It *needs* us to be afraid of it," said Charley. "That's how the Hobb-Hound gets its power – from fear! It *feeds* on vengeance, hate and fright, just like the rhyme says."

"But at the end of the day, the Hobb-Hound is just a bully," said Billy. "And if you stand up to a bully…"

"I'm not afraid of you!" said Major Smallbone, all his military training coming into practice. Chest out, shoulders back, moustache at attention.

"I'm not, neither," yelled Hawkins at the top of his voice.

"Nor me!" shouted Fraser.

"Give us back our children and leave this town at once!" demanded Coldblood.

The Hobb-Hound was quivering. The short hairs which covered its body were prickling. Instead of growing fat on fear, the demon was shrinking. Its head was low to the ground now, its tail between its legs…

"We're not afraid!" shouted Charley.

A growl rose from the Hobb-Hound's throat, full of menace and the promise of violence. Although the Hobb-Hound's body was growing smaller, its hatred was not.

The zoetrope still spun, magical sparks shooting off

it like lightning bolts. "You might have found some courage to stand up to me," said the Hobb-Hound. "But *Parker* is still terrified!"

Parker said nothing. He stood there, silent, head bowed.

"Tell it," urged Charley, wheeling her chair over to the broken mirror so she could be beside him. "Tell it you aren't afraid."

"But he is," said the Hobb-Hound. "Parker has *always* been a frightened little boy…a yellow-belly…a chicken heart."

Parker said nothing, but Charley thought she noticed a subtle change in his stance. Charley took his hand and held it hard…

"Weakling, namby-pamby, coward, cry baby…" the Hobb-Hound taunted.

"I'm not," said Parker softly.

"Oh, but you are! You will NEVER stop feeling afraid," the Hobb-Hound mocked. "Once a coward, *always* a coward."

Billy walked over to stand beside Charley and Parker. The raw meat stench of the Hobb-Hound's breath washed over them but they stood their ground. "He's not afraid," said Billy.

"I'm not going to let you bully me any more," said Parker, a new edge to his voice.

The Hobb-Hound flinched, as if in pain. "Yes, you are!"

"No," said Patrick Parker, firmly and clearly. "I AM NOT!"

The Hobb-Hound drew back, as if Parker's confidence had hit it like a punch on the nose.

"It stops tonight!" shouted Parker. "I may not be able to prevent you from taking my soul, but I won't give you the pleasure of spending one more second of my life being scared of you!"

"Well said, Parker!" encouraged Major Smallbone. "That's the spirit!"

Bunny edged forward too. "We're not afraid!"

The Hobb-Hound snapped its jaws and barked, but now it sounded like a cornered animal and instead of making Parker cower, it gave its former victim *more* strength.

"I'M NOT AFRAID!" shouted Parker.

"It's working," said Charley, remembering the line from the ancient manuscript. "'*Do not let your hearts be troubled. Do not be afraid. When the dark dog draws near, a courageous soul shall cast out fear!*'"

And now Major Smallbone added his voice. "We're not afraid of you!"

And Coldblood. And Hawkins. And Fraser. "We're not afraid of you!"

Until they were all shouting with one voice: *"WE ARE NOT AFRAID OF YOU!"*

"The Hobb-Hound's power is fading," yelled Charley, as the demon dog continued to shrivel up before their eyes. "We've beaten it!"

"But it's not over yet!" warned Billy. "The Hobb-Hound is so weak, it's lost control of the zoetrope!"

"Isn't that a good thing?" said Charley.

"I'm not so sure," said Billy. "Look!"

As if to prove Billy's point, bolts of magical lightning flashed and crashed through the battered tent as the zoetrope spun. Billy ducked as one bolt passed within inches of his head, close enough to singe his hair. It struck the tent wall instead, burning a smoking hole in the canvas.

"The whole tent might go up in smoke," gasped Bunny. The central spindle which supported the whole framework was starting to smoulder as the friction grew. The wheel juddered uncontrollably. More sparks flew.

At the heart of the zoetrope, in the dead centre of the magical storm, a dark hole appeared. It was as if a piece of the night sky had been brought down to earth. And the darkness was expanding.

"The dimensional gate is opening," said Billy. "Everyone grab hold of something! Quick!"

The wind was whipping up inside the tent, swirling round and round in time with the zoetrope. The broken shards of mirror lifted from the ground and were sucked away, like a flurry of sparkling hail. The sheets and curtains which had covered the mirrors were picked up and dragged towards the middle of the spinning wheel.

The Hobb-Hound, which had shrivelled to the size of a wolf, made a chuckling sound and seemed to regain some strength. "Scary, isn't it?!"

Billy grasped one of the tent poles with both hands as the whirlwind shrieked round the tent. Coldblood wrapped his arms around another tent pole just in time. Thinking quickly, Charley had tied herself and her wheelchair to one of the two main tent poles with her belt. Her teeth were gritted against the spectral wind and her long red hair streamed out behind her.

"Grab hands," said Billy. "We're not losing anyone else!"

All of the others managed to link up in a human chain, with Coldblood, the shortest and the fattest, acting as the anchor. He was the only one with both feet still on the ground. Fraser was beside him, his arms locked in a bear hug around the vicar's waist. Hawkins was next in line. He had a double-handed grip on Fraser's belt. Hawkins's arms were stretched out straight and his body was horizontal with the floor, held aloft by the whirlwind. Major Smallbone was next, clinging to Hawkins's ankle with one hand and holding his daughter with the other. Bunny and the major were flapping in the wind like a sheet on the washing line. "Hold on, Bunny!" the major shouted above the rushing of the wind. "Hold on!"

Billy's legs were in the air too now. His arms screamed with pain as he clung to the tent pole, afraid that at any moment they might be ripped from their sockets by the force of the vortex. There was nothing he could do...and the Hobb-Hound was growing again, lapping up their feelings of doom, and drinking in their terror.

Bunny's position was the most dangerous of all, close to the gaping vortex, magical lightning flashing all around her. Her father's hand was the only thing still keeping her in this world. Billy could hardly bear to watch. If the major's fingers slipped...

Then Billy realized that someone was missing. Where was Parker? Had he slipped out of the tent and left them?

Had he really been a coward like the Hobb-Hound had said?

A flash of movement told Billy that he had been wrong.

Parker had managed to lash himself to the mechanical Grim Reaper but, as Billy watched, he saw Parker untie himself. There was stony determination in the man's eyes. "This ends here," said Parker and, using every scrap of strength in his body, the small man launched himself at the Hobb-Hound from behind.

Caught by surprise, the Hobb-Hound lost its footing and sprawled forward. Parker wasn't *physically* strong enough to hurt the demon, or even to scratch it. But, Billy realized, Parker's raw courage hit the Hobb-Hound like a hammer blow. The demon actually yelped as Parker stood up to it for the first time. Parker saw the glint of fear in the Hobb-Hound's eyes and threw himself at the creature again, locking his arms around its neck, and then dragging them *both* – man *and* demon – towards the swirling vortex of the gateway.

The Hobb-Hound fought back, but its wings were tattered shreds and as Parker's bravery grew, the Hound's evil power was collapsing. A grim tug of war began, with Parker doing everything he could to pull the

Hobb-Hound *into* the vortex, and the demon tugging to get away. The demon howled and spat and snarled, but Parker refused to let go. Even the red blaze of its hideous eyes was growing dim. The Hobb-Hound lashed out in desperation, trying to hook its claws into something – *anything* – which it could hang on to. Its evil eyes fixed greedily onto Bunny, and Billy could almost read its mind…if it could grab one of Bunny's flailing legs…

Parker must have seen it too, because just as the Hobb-Hound's grasping claws lunged towards her, Parker kicked the demon's back legs out from underneath it. The Hobb-Hound scrabbled madly to regain its grip, but the whirlwind lifted it from the floor with Parker still clinging to its back.

"Checkmate!" shouted Parker triumphantly.

The Hobb-Hound was as helpless as a spider in the toilet when the flush has been pulled. And just like a spider in a toilet, the demon dog was spun round and round as the vortex swept it in. With a final terrifying roar, the Hobb-Hound disappeared through the gateway, sucked into the prison it had created. Taking Patrick Parker with it.

# CHAPTER TWENTY-SEVEN

# OUT OF THE SHADOWS

As Parker and the Hobb-Hound finally vanished from sight, the zoetrope slowed and the wind dropped.

Billy fell to the floor and lay there. He was drained mentally and physically, but he still had a job to do. He was a S.C.R.E.A.M. detective and this case wasn't shut until the kidnapped boys were reunited with their families. Billy climbed back to his feet and stood unsteadily. Everyone inside the tent was sprawled on the floor, completely exhausted after their brush with death. Charley was untying herself from the tent pole. Quickly she wheeled over to Billy.

She whispered to him, keen for the others not to hear. "I thought the boys would be released from the wheel when the Hobb-Hound took their place," she said.

"Me too," said Billy. "Any ideas?"

"Show me where the contract is written on the zoetrope, Billy. Perhaps there's a clue there."

The zoetrope was still intact in spite of all the destruction caused by the storm, although the clockwork reaper was smashed beyond repair. Billy lit the candle he kept in his satchel. Together they went over and peered underneath the wheel, Charley reading the words that were written there in Parker's blood. She shook her head. "It isn't any language that I recognize. We could copy it down and then I can ask Sparkwell about it, work on a translation. But that's going to take time."

"Time we don't have."

The others were stirring. Checking themselves for broken bones. "What happened?" said Bunny.

"The Hobb-Hound has gone," said Charley. "Parker sacrificed himself to save us all."

"I think that's the bravest thing I've ever seen," said Bunny.

Charley looked at the zoetrope, then back at Billy, a sparkle in her eyes.

"You know something, don't you?" said Billy.

"It's just a theory," said Charley. "But if we think that the zoetrope is actually some kind of prayer wheel—"

"A *curse* wheel, more like, but I know what you mean," Billy continued. "Each time it spins the incantation written on the inside is activated."

"Exactly. So what if we spin the wheel in the *opposite* direction?"

"We reverse the curse?"

"That's what I'm hoping," said Charley.

The four members of the Chess Club were watching, huddled together in shock, not having the words to explain the last half-hour of their lives. At last, Major Smallbone found his voice.

"Where is Arthur?" he asked. "Where are our boys?"

"Arthur's still in here," said Billy, as he took hold of the zoetrope and tried to push it in the reverse direction. It didn't budge. "Don't just stand there, gents, lend a hand."

The men joined Billy and combined their strength, heaving until the zoetrope started to spin.

After the bombardment of noise they had endured, the silence inside the tent hung thick and heavy on the cold night air. They all watched and waited.

"Arthur!" gasped Bunny, as the first silhouette appeared. It was working! Thank God!

The zoetrope whirled and the shadow of Arthur Smallbone was joined by the silhouettes of three more boys.

"Look," said Billy. "They aren't running any more."

"And there's no big black dog nipping at their heels," added Charley.

As they watched, another figure joined the boys; it was the silhouette of a man.

"That's Parker," said Bunny, a smile tweaking at the corner of her lips as her hope rose.

The zoetrope continued to twirl. The atmosphere inside the battered tent was tense. Coldblood was praying. Fraser was chewing nervously on his lip. Major Smallbone was plucking at his moustache. "I can't bear this," the major gasped. "We're so close but our boys are *still* inside that blasted contraption!"

Before their eyes they saw the silhouettes huddle together as if they were having a conversation between themselves. The silhouette of Parker cupped his hands and held them out like a stirrup. Arthur Smallbone's silhouette put his foot in Parker's hands and then Parker gave him a bunk-up so that Arthur could get a finger grip on the top of the spinning zoetrope, as if it were a wall.

"Come on, son!" yelled Major Smallbone. "You can do it!"

Charley found that she was holding her breath as Arthur's silhouette actually emerged from the zoetrope. "Scientifically this simply isn't possible," she said, as Arthur's shadow sat on top of the zoetrope, legs dangling.

Arthur Smallbone was there...and he wasn't.

The shadow was Arthur-sized and Arthur-shaped. But the resemblance stopped there. Arthur had no physical form – he remained a black outline.

The shadow Arthur reached down from his perch and hauled up the next boy to sit beside him.

"Fred!" said Mr Hawkins.

Then Herbert Fraser and Sidney Coldblood scrabbled up, helped by Arthur and Fred from above and Parker from below. Only when all four kidnapped boys were sitting on top of their former prison did Parker haul himself up beside them.

"It's incredible," said Major Smallbone, shaking his head. "I don't understand anything that has happened this evening."

"You don't have to understand," said Billy with relief.

"Just get ready to welcome your boys home."

Arthur Smallbone slid gracefully down the side of the zoetrope and landed on solid ground, quickly followed by the other shadow boys and the silhouette of Parker.

Billy's heart sank.

When their feet reached the floor the boys did not become flesh and blood again. They remained as shadows; flat, black, two-dimensional and as silent as the grave.

The shadow that was Arthur slid across the floor to Bunny and the major. Bunny reached for her brother but her hand passed straight through him. Arthur's shadow arm stretched, long and thin, travelling up his sister's body until his hand rested on the soft pale skin of her cheek like a black bruise. "No," Bunny gasped. "This is too horrible."

The other shadow boys hesitated. They were no longer trapped inside their prison, but they weren't free. Sidney's shadow approached the Reverend Coldblood. The boy's hand brushed his father's fingers but there was no comfort there. Then Sidney's shadow retreated too, gliding across the floor, as insubstantial as a ghost.

All four shadow boys slid up the canvas wall of the tent and gave the impression that they were standing upright in a line, beside the shadow of Parker. With a sadness so heavy that Billy could almost touch it, the boys waved slowly and then, one by one, slid back down the wall, under the canvas and away into the night.

Bunny Smallbone started to cry. "We've lost them."

"I'm sorry," said Billy. "This isn't how it's meant to end."

The silence was suffocating; a toxic mixture of confusion, disappointment and grief. The men looked devastated. Bunny bit her fist as she fought against the terrible wave of sorrow which threatened to sweep her away.

Suddenly Bunny gulped. Charley had an icy feeling in the pit of her stomach – the zoetrope was starting to spin again.

"No!" said Bunny. "Please, I can't take any more!"

A new silhouette could be seen inside the zoetrope. Not a boy. It was a creature with the body of a man, the wings of a bat and the head of a massive dog: the Hobb-Hound.

"It's starting all over again," gasped Major Smallbone.

The zoetrope revolved and the Hobb-Hound ran. Round and round and round. "Don't speak too soon," said Billy. "It looks like the demon is trapped inside its own prison."

"Good," said Bunny. "I want my revenge."

"We don't do revenge," said Charley softly. "We do justice."

"My brother is still lost," said Bunny. "Where's the justice in that?"

Just then there was a noise outside the tent. Footsteps approaching and muttering voices. Charley drew her revolver. "Stand behind me," she ordered, training her gun on the tent flap.

"Do as she says," snapped Billy, looking for a weapon of his own.

"Who could it be?" said Bunny, clinging to Billy's arm.

"I don't know," said Billy. "But with everything that we've been through I think we'd better be safe than sorry."

The voices seemed less threatening as they got closer, more childlike. They were right outside now, whoever they were. The tent flap was thrown open…and Charley took her finger off the trigger as four boys and a man rushed inside. Arthur Smallbone, Fred Hawkins, Herbert Fraser, Sidney Coldblood and Patrick Parker. They looked tired, dishevelled and hungry. But very happy to be alive.

"How?" Major Smallbone mumbled.

"Would it help if I say it was supernatural?" said Billy.

"Not really," said the major. "But it doesn't matter how, does it? All that matters is that our sons have come back to us."

"Bunny!" Arthur yelled and ran straight into his sister's arms.

# CHAPTER TWENTY-EIGHT

# A Man's Best Friend

"Tell me again," said Constable Dunstable, shaking his head.

"It's really very simple," said Charley with a sparkle. "One of the illusions at the carnival was extremely realistic, and the audience became hysterical and ran riot."

"Hysterical," Dunstable repeated doubtfully. "Right. But what caused all the damage? The carnival is flattened."

"You'd never guess," Billy laughed, "but some silly lads put a bull in a fancy-dress costume and then let it loose, saying it was the Hobb-Hound. But you'd have to be a complete idiot to believe that!"

"A bull," said Constable Dunstable. "Right. Well, that makes perfect sense to me."

"And the boys are all back, safe and sound," Charley reminded him.

"That's true enough," said Constable Dunstable. "But kidnapping is still kidnapping, and I must uphold the law. You can talk to the prisoner for ten minutes," he said, closing the cell door with a clang.

Patrick Parker sat quietly. He looked like a different man, Charley thought. He wasn't wearing his Dr Vindicta disguise for a start, but it was much more than that; a deeper change had happened.

"You really *aren't* afraid any more, are you?" said Charley.

"I've wasted so many years being scared," said Parker.

"Like you told the Hobb-Hound," said Charley. "That time is over."

"There's still one thing I don't understand though," said Billy. "How did you meet the Hobb-Hound in the first place?"

"It's a long story," said Parker.

"Think you can manage it in ten minutes?"

Parker lifted his face towards the cell window,

enjoying the warmth of the sun through the bars. "I was heartbroken after I lost my apprenticeship. I had no family, no one to help me and so after my time at Milverton Hall was finished I was out in the world on my own."

"That must have been lonely," said Charley.

"It was," said Parker. "I walked and walked, day after day. I was a tramp I suppose, setting up camp wherever I could, sometimes catching a rabbit for supper, but mostly going hungry. I was a very frightened young man. Lonely, too." Parker sighed. "At first, when the black dog started to follow me I thought it was my imagination."

Charley nodded. "It was drawn to you by the scent of fear."

"I suppose it must have been, looking back, but at the time I was grateful for it. For the first few days it followed at a distance. It stopped when I stopped, walked when I walked. I started to call it 'Shadow' because it was always behind me and each night when I cooked my meal I looked out for it. I even started leaving bowls of stew out in the hope of tempting Shadow closer." He gave a half-smile. "I thought we were kindred spirits."

"Why?" asked Billy.

"Shadow seemed afraid of me too, as if he had been treated badly and needed to build up trust again."

"The same as you."

"Exactly," said Parker. "So, night after night I did everything I could to try and get Shadow to come and sit by my fire. I was so happy when he first took food from my hand. And when Shadow stayed by my fire for the whole night sleeping by my side, well…I thought that my life was getting better at last.

"It sounds ridiculous, I know, but it was wonderful to have a companion after feeling alone for so long. We walked side by side, we played in the woods, looked after each other. And I talked to Shadow. I told him everything…"

"About the Chess Club and the apprenticeship."

"And about how I felt inside. The sadness. The fear. One night I remember that I had been crying and I was stroking Shadow. 'You're my only friend in the world,' I said. And then Shadow replied with the voice of a man, '*I know.*'"

"Didn't you run a mile?" said Billy. "I think I would've."

"To be honest," said Parker, "I thought the voice was

in my head. By the time the Hobb-Hound had control of me, it was too late. Then Shadow told me I could get my own back if I signed the contract..." He shrugged. "And, well, you know the rest."

"What will you do now?" asked Charley. "After your trial, I mean."

"After *prison*, you mean. I've been thinking about that," said Parker. "I might settle down in Hobb's End, open up the little watch shop that I've always dreamed of. I've got enough money set aside from the carnival. I won't be going back to it. That's for sure."

Constable Dunstable appeared at the cell door and opened it with a rattle of keys. "Right then, let's be having you."

Billy and Charley made for the door. "I will speak with the judge," said Charley. "If I explain, I'm certain he'll be merciful."

"No need for that, Detective Steel," said Constable Dunstable. "You're free to go, Parker."

"What do you mean?"

"None of the kidnapped boys' fathers want to press charges," said the constable.

Parker smiled, a big broad smile. "Ten minutes exactly," he said, looking at his father's gold watch.

"A much shorter sentence than I was expecting."

Constable Dunstable coughed disapprovingly. "And don't let it happen again!"

# The Ghost of a Chance

The sun was setting over Hobb's End. The early evening air had a cold, crisp edge, but the two S.C.R.E.A.M. detectives were both cosy and warm. There were two reasons for that: the satisfying glow that came when they solved a case, and the enormous fire burning in front of them.

"But what I don't understand is how the boys changed from being shadows to being real again," said Charley. She had brought some marshmallows with her and a toasting fork. She brought the sweet sticky mess to her lips and took a gooey bite.

"It was a delayed reaction," Billy explained. "Parker's bravery robbed the Hobb-Hound of its strength, and as the demon's power grew weaker, so its control over the boys faded."

It was Billy's turn to pluck a marshmallow from the fork. He popped it into his mouth whole. "Job well done," he grinned.

"The case of the Carnival of Monsters is solved," Charley said with satisfaction.

"Almost," said Billy. "We have to wait for this fire to die down first."

The zoetrope was burning nicely. Now they had saved Hobb's End from its demon, they didn't want to be responsible for burning the place to the ground.

Billy was sitting on a sturdy wooden chest. He patted it affectionately. "Luther had it sent from London on the night train. It's made from yew wood and lined with lead."

"Nice and safe then," said Charley.

"Exactly. As soon as the zoetrope is reduced to ashes we can gather up the remains and lock them away in here where they can't do any harm. The Hobb-Hound won't be coming back to Hobb's End any time soon."

"Good work, partner," said Charley. She gave a tired

sigh. "It's been a busy couple of days though, hardly a relaxing break in the country."

"You'll be even more pleased to get back to London when you see this, then," said Billy, handing her an advert cut from a newspaper.

"From Luther, I suppose?"

Billy nodded.

Charley read aloud.

## FOR SALE
### SIX LIVE GHOSTS
5 pounds each (or near offer).
Available from 13 Hanging Sword
Alley, LONDON EC4.
Ask for Mr Raven.
(No time-wasters please.)

"It sounds like we've got a new case."

"Here we go again, Duchess."

# THE END

# ACKNOWLEDGEMENTS

Writing is the best fun you can have with imaginary friends. I have some real friends too, though, and I'd like to mention some of them now.

My Usborne friends continue to add enormously to the joy of creating these books. Rebecca Hill – thank you for your ongoing support. Manuel Šumberac and Will Steele – thank you for another stunning cover; you guys really spoil me! Anne Finnis and Helen Greathead – thank you so much for your skilful editing and your wise and witty comments... we've got the band back together! Stephanie King – special thanks for being such an incredible and inspirational editor; I take my hat off to you. No really. That's not a metaphor. I mean my real hat.

Congratulations to Khulan Stevens, who entered a competition with the Reading Agency and ended up as a human cannonball!

Darling Jules – my best friend, always. Ben – thank you for being my first reader and a truly amazing son. Lucy – thank you for inventing Dynamite (!) and for being a wonderful daughter in every way. Mam and Jack – thanks for your support. Mum and Dad – thank you for all the bedtime stories; you really started something there!

Father, thank you for everything.